AND SOMETIMES THEY WIN

ERIC RABIN

ISBN: 0692827587
ISBN 13: 9780692827581

Monsters are real, and ghosts are too,
They live inside us,
And sometimes they win.

—Edgar Allen Poe

Reverse Tell:
In poker, a deliberate action made by a player to convey the opposite of whatever information that action might appear to convey

REVERSE TELL

Here's something you may not know. Success in poker is often predicated on deception. As in, I'll tell you a story that I want you to believe. I'll do this to coax a desired action from you. Put more chips in a pot, or perhaps prevent you from doing so. If I'm able to deceive successfully, that means I've swayed you to act in my own best interests, and not your own. Hey, I need money to live, just like anyone else.

At least I'm truthful about being deceptive, right? I should get a few points for that. Here, with you now, my aim is pure and sincere. To introduce you to a strange, dark world and detail my place in it. To help you see what you've probably never seen. Or might never have the opportunity to see for yourself. My little gift to you.

Or maybe I have a hidden agenda. And there's some more sinister reason for telling you all of this, opening up my twisted life to you. Could be. I don't know. I'm really trying hard to be sincere here. Yet maybe I'm still deluding myself after all these years that I actually have a grasp on how things are. Or *why* they are as they are. As if I'm capable of shedding light on the many obscurities surrounding me. I always thought it was a worthy pursuit—to acquire some coveted skill and then use it for gain in various life settings. Have I been wrong about this the whole time? I can't be sure. Getting the proper perspective on all this is tough when you're still *at sixes and sevens*, as the Brits might say. Obviously, I've still got some things to work out.

An expert poker player deceives to attain a goal. I think I'm considered an expert, but I'm not sure. Is that humility or just a sneaky way to gain your trust by first undercutting the very skill I'm supposed to possess? See? There I go again. Force of habit, I guess. Such is and will be our relationship. My apologies, but you'll get used to it.

I am a poker player. Here's my story...

"Cómo? Qué es lo que me estás contando?"

Isabella. Her name was Isabella. She lay beside Marco under the covers, perplexed. Her English was spotty (a generous assessment, he thought), though *she's* the one who asked *him* to tell her some interesting story in English. Not to torture herself, he can only assume, but maybe just to hear the accent and delivery of his own native tongue. She didn't understand, and asked Marco in her sleepy Argentina-tinged voice what he'd been saying to her.

"Cosas interesantes, princesa. Duérmete." *Interesting things*, he told her. *Go to sleep.*

The room was on the fourth floor of Commerce Casino in Los Angeles. Hours earlier, Marco was five hours deep into a high-limit poker game at one of the tables below, on the first floor. He had been bored to distraction and getting crushed, and if not for a touch of serendipity, he might have ripped through another five hours with much of the same. Instead, his old poker pal Freddie swooped in like some benevolent hawk, grabbing a fistful of his black T-shirt and telling him in no uncertain terms, *Yo, follow me...let's go*, as they shot off into the boisterousness of the lobby bar, its air a heady mix of french fries and whiskey, where Isabella and her older sister sat already several drinks in, another half-empty glass in front of each. *You're a good man, Freddie*, he thought. *And your timing's impeccable.*

Back upstairs, Marco realized he had probably tossed down a few more cocktails than expected, a thick haze now surrounding the details of the hours that followed. How'd they get to the room? Where did Freddie and the other girl go? *Eh...so there's a few gaps. Big deal.* He turned on his side. *Ah, a certainty.* There she lay—the beautiful young Argentine, with her long tumble of silky, chestnut-colored hair, curled up beside him now in bed. And yet, despite his good fortune and the way his weary body sank like a leaden rag doll into the mattress, the possibility of a headache couldn't be ruled out entirely. *Strange...I never get headaches. Dehydrated? Wiped out from all the travel, maybe?* He noticed the air-conditioning was blasting at least two dial clicks too high but flinched at the mere thought of getting out from under the covers. Instead, he opted for the easy, lazy solution, which meant snuggling up close to Isabella, as they simultaneously stole and gifted each other's body heat. The room was dark except for a dim-red neon glare reflected in a thin slice of the window, the only part left exposed by starchy gray curtains that seemed as old as Marco himself. Marco closed his eyes and breathed in deep. She smelled of fresh-cut lilacs. Or was it gardenias?

He turned on his back and looked up. He found himself staring at the ceiling longer than someone in bed should ever stare at any ceiling. It wasn't like there was anything interesting up there to see. A couple of shadowy pocks in the drywall, or gypsum board, or whatever the hell they called it. Was that an *insect*? Nope, just a shadow. He spun over once again, frustrated at how this ridiculous activity came at the expense of quality, sound sleep. He felt he might be drilling a hole in the sheets somehow from all his turning. Maybe down into the mattress too. *Gimme another few minutes, and I might carve out a pretty little design in the goddamn bed frame.* He let out a sigh.

Isabella was out cold, oblivious to his plight and mounting frustration. *I wonder if her sister knows where she is,* Marco thought idly. *I'm sure she's not too worried.* Another long, slow, deep breath. Same floral scent. He turned onto his other side with a slight groan. The same red glare in the window. Thankfully, the headache never showed up, but insomnia had certainly crept in, howling now like a pack of hungry, moon-lit wolves. At this point, it seemed the choice of whether to go back downstairs wasn't really that much of a choice. It was that, or play connect the ceiling dots. He groped about on the floor, searching for his clothes, trying desperately to not make a sound. He gave himself a B+ on the overall result, as a metal button clinked against something. Now dressed, he cracked open the door and then nudged it closed behind him with a soft click.

The hallways were lined with grubby dark-red carpets and faded hunter-green wallpaper. Marco tapped the elevator button with a distracted thumb, musing about the evening's events. In his left front pocket, he jiggled a half dozen or so chips worth roughly twenty thousand dollars in total. *Round two at the tables*, he thought idly. He caught his reflection in an oval wall-mounted mirror and saw the night's work staring back at him: his usual semichaotic spiky hair had turned full-blown riotous; smudges of burgundy lipstick dappled the skin around his high cheekbones; his lower lip showed a line of dried, crusty blood, which he knew was the result of an earlier Isabella love bite; three-day-old scruff had turned into four. He quickly rubbed off the lipstick with the back of his hand and licked away the dried blood. Then he scratched the top area of his new tattoo on his upper shoulder, where a red-and-yellow triangle peeked out from the collar of his black John Varvatos V-neck T-shirt. An elevator dinged open, and he stepped in, massaging his temples on the way down to the lobby.

His mind drifted off to memories of his first autumn in Miami two years earlier. Marco had worked as a pool server at the Delano, one of the swankiest hotels in the country. Famous actors, musicians, models, rich businessmen—this is where they went to break away and be seen among other rich and famous people whose goal (like theirs) was to bask in the sunshine and spend obscene heaps of money. Pop open top-flight champagne and toss back tequila shots at 10:00 a.m. on a

Tuesday at the pool, lined with plush white lounge chairs and manicured palm trees.

Marco recalled the dorky white outfit they made all the pool employees wear. Sure, the hotel facade was a pristine white, as was the elegant interior decked out with spotless white couches along the walls of the lobby and gauzy white curtains that billowed with gusts of Atlantic Ocean air. So all-white outfits made sense. But it was the overly tight white shorts and T-shirts that got to him. Along with the white belt and white socks and white sneakers and white fisherman's hat (fortunately optional). The way the unremitting sun would bear down for hours on the exposed arms and legs and necks and faces of all the pool employees and toast those parts to a deep-brown crisp. White-clad parts would obviously remain largely or altogether untanned, creating a humorous nude-in-front-of-the-mirror effect. The consensus was that they were made to look dorky so that the rich and famous patrons would shine that much brighter in their excessively fashionable pool attire, especially when side by side the employees. It seemed to work.

"Do you have any idea how white my ass looks?" Nicole, a fellow pool server, had asked him one scorching afternoon.

"Um, you are aware G-strings are legal here in South Beach, yes? As in, after work, or on days off?" Marco had wondered why she didn't mention her boobs, which had to be equally pale.

"Yeah, well *you* go lie out on the hot sand after baking in the sun here all week."

"Here, let's compare butt cheek color."

"Maybe later." She winked and sped off to deliver a fresh bucket of ice for a champagne-swigging pop-music star known the world over.

Marco's manager at the pool was one Ivan Parker, as he tended to introduce himself. About average height, with olive skin and dark curly hair, he showed a professional demeanor around the pool but acted like just one of the crew behind the scenes. He and Marco hit it off from the get-go. More than a few times after work, the two went somewhere local to grab a few drinks. One fateful late afternoon, wrapping up a shift early at the pool because of an outright deluge, Ivan had invited Marco to join him for a *cool one* in the managers' office.

"Hey, there's a matter I wanna discuss, bud. An opportunity. To maybe really change things for you, I mean. Not sure if you're interested, but let's go chat a bit..."

He wondered how different his life might be had he not hung around to listen.

Marco snapped back to the present. Los Angeles. Commerce Casino. Two a.m. Poker table. Twenty/forty no-limit hold 'em table. Twenty-five-hundred-dollar minimum buy-in, no max. Isabella snoozing away upstairs, dreaming of strange adventures in a strange land. Down here, Lady Luck was smiling at him, grinning ear to fucking...yesssssss! Nice. Big. Fat. Pot. Marco's facial expression barely changed, but inside he was dancing a sweet little jig. He knew for sure on that flop that if he slowplayed his set and made himself look weak early in the hand, maybe Hollywooded a bit, that he could induce the old rich dude in seat three to bet the turn big. Then Marco could just check-raise jam, and the dupe would put in his remaining stack, thinking his aces or kings were still good. *Poetry in motion*, he thought. Up $7,200. *Christ, will this come in handy.*

Marco sat around for another fifteen to twenty minutes to make a good show of things, which any poker player knew was instead really just subtle gamesmanship. As in, Marco had no intention of playing longer than that, or giving anyone at the table a chance to maybe get lucky and cut into his winnings for the session. So he'd stack his chips and splash around in another small pot or two, knowing full well that he was about to quit the game. Maybe he'd fake a text from Isabella upstairs— *Oh hey, gotta run guys. Young lady upstairs is asking for me. Nice playing with everyone.* Then just shoot off to the cage, hop back in the elevator, and snuggle up next to his new Latina friend, now warm under the sheets.

As he got ready to leave, Marco surveyed the space in front of him, chips stacked in neat rows pushed up against the table's black-vinyl, foam-padded edge. Looking directly at all this money forced him to struggle with his thoughts again. He felt a sudden and uncontrollable urge to call out to Isabella in his head:

Bella, maybe I should tell your precious sleeping form a touch more about me. For my sake, really—just to get it off my chest; help squeeze it clear from my psyche. Talking to you earlier helped me feel better, and like before, I don't need you to respond, just listen. Like some sort of telepathic, proxy psychiatrist, I guess—one whose silence and sympathetic ear will let me come up with the answers to my own questions.

I'll start where I left off, more or less. I used to be a professional poker player. Before everything that happened. I guess you could say it was fun while it lasted. Not to mention profitable.

I used to enjoy saying it. The sweet-sounding, alliterative, percussive pop that snapped off my lips like minifirecrackers. Professional poker player. Pop. Pop. Pop. Like little BBs poking holes through a paper carnival target. Pop. Pop. Pop.

But things are much different now. I'm different now.

Sure I'm here for a few days at a casino, putting in some time at the tables (and how fortunate was I to meet you, princess), but it's sort of like a necessary break from everything, closer really to a vacation of the mind and spirit. I still enjoy the game—not like I once did, maybe never will again—but I can no longer rely on chance and good fortune to carry me through. There are money and debt concerns to consider. Plus, I don't know, maybe the skills I've honed in poker have led me to do things I wouldn't have done otherwise. Maybe they're the source of many of my troubles, my uneasy conscience.

Like I said, things are different now.

That $7,200 profit at this table, right here—I'm not certain I can even consider it to be mine. Sure, I won it legally and fairly, and in a state-licensed and regulated casino. And though I used deceptive tactics to get it, that's what your garden-variety, clash-of-wits poker game is all about. So we can agree the $7,200 was legitimately won, right? But what about the pressing debts I might have or what I have to repay? Is that money still mine?

What about the twenty thousand worth of chips that rattled in my pocket before I sat down? Was this even mine? Is money loaned to you yours? Or just temporarily in your possession until repaid. What if you successfully acquire a sum of money by illegal means? Theft or fraud, say. Yours? What, until you get caught? How about by legal, but ethically questionable, largely duplicitous means—would you call that money yours? Why? Did you earn it, somehow? Sounds iffy, if we're being honest with each other. But so, back to the original point—the $27,000 plus in my pocket and in front of me at the table. Whose is it? Can I even call it mine?

And sure, Bella, money is important in many ways, but what about virtue? A sense of right and wrong? Should these qualities take a backseat to living a cushy-type lifestyle? Shouldn't a person be guided instead by doing the right thing over doing what's in his or her best financial interest—and not let the lust for money steer the ship? These are the questions that plague me these days. I could certainly use some answers. I just wish there were some easy way for me to reconcile what I've done with the virtuous, compassionate person I try to be, had made solemn promises to be. Promises I may have broken along the way. Along with relationships I may have helped destroy. Horrible things I may have done. I can't pretend to ignore all this. And so then, I ask—is the money still mine? All my possessions? What about this uneasy form of happiness? Do I even deserve any of it?

As I've said, things are different now. I'm different now.

I wouldn't burden you with a Spanish translation of this whole crazed, emotional outpouring. Too messy for you, really. Again, this was all for me. Thanks for listening, princess. Maybe I'll even get some damn sleep.

———

Midafternoon the next day, Marco sped off in his black Chevy Charger rental car through the gray, desolate streets and smog-choked air to a Peet's Coffee ten minutes from the casino, his bags still unpacked in the hotel room. Isabella had left to go out somewhere with her sister. Shopping, she'd said. He thought he might check out the following morning, return the rental and grab the next flight—the next, agonizingly long flight—back home. He was sick of traveling by now, with Los Angeles his last stop, and merely wanted to spend the rest of his short time in LA alone, sipping a nice dark roast with his feet propped up, reading a novel he'd been halfway through since forever. A whim which—fortunately for Marco on this particular day—the gentle sun and cool breeze out by the cafe's patio had been nice enough to accommodate.

He drifted off a few times with the book in his lap, and in his dreamy state, he recalled bits and pieces of a brief table conversation from earlier the day before. Just a thirty-second exchange, but long enough, it seemed, to aptly reflect a key part of his life now.

"Girlfriend nagging ya?" another player had asked him, a few seats over at the same table, after Marco had ignored a series of buzzes from his cell. Marco considered the question. He wasn't really concerned about any nagging—it went way beyond that. Closer actually to...*to what?* he mused.

A few seconds passed, and he knew he had to respond to the guy. "Uh, could be," said Marco. "Don't feel like chatting on the phone right now. I haven't even looked."

"You two live on the East Coast?" This gentleman was apparently eager to exploit the *on the phone* loophole from Marco's response.

"Huh? Uh, yeah, something like that. Long story." Marco fished out a pair of stringy black headphones from his front pocket and set about untangling a few stubborn knots. Maybe now the guy would pick up on the *long-story-with-no-other-information-forthcoming* part of the sentence. He looked back over in the direction of Mr. Chatty, who seemed affronted somehow. Was that *really* the guy Marco had become? The dude was only trying to connect with him. Marco took another deep breath, rubbed his tired eyes and swallowed hard. "Sorry, man. Another time, maybe."

PREFLOP

Four of a Kind:
Four cards of a same number or value

FOUR OF A KIND

Unlike *the rain in Spain*, which (Marco fondly remembered his mom's singsong voice as a kid) *falls mainly on the plain*, there in South Florida it fell anywhere and everywhere. Thick, punishing curtains of rain doled out by dark puffy clouds. Even at the famous Delano Hotel it rained. Sometimes for just five brutal minutes. Other times longer. And so poolside festivities were occasionally interrupted.

Marco decided to utilize this time productively. Not in the sense necessarily that Ivan or the assistant manager, Brian, had in mind: clean the stations, fold some napkins, cut some fruit for the bar, and the like. No, Marco liked to read a book or listen to a podcast, maybe expand his mind a bit on matters that interested him, while waiting to see what the skies ultimately decided to do.

This late autumn day's extended rain dump afforded him the pleasure. Nestled cozily in a cushioned chair, set in an out-of-the-way corner, Marco plunged into a talk about *quantum jumping*, a fascinating topic that Ivan would also sit in on, as Marco had forgotten his headphones and the speaker volume was turned up high to compete with the pounding raindrops.

…so again, it's essentially the process by which someone envisions a desired result or state of being that is different from an existing situation…and by clearly observing that possibility and supplying it sufficient energy, one can make a leap into that alternate reality…

"Like this stuff, huh, Marcsy?"

"Yeah, Ivan, especially when I can hear it. Shhhh."

…and the idea behind it is that we live in a multiverse of parallel universes, which usually have no connection to one another. Quantum jumping could be considered a kind of handshake through time and space—a certain connection that forms a bridge that allows one to physically end up in another reality. To the universe, both of "you" still exist, but your awareness of who you are merges in one reality, leaving the other behind. Think of it as…

"What ya guys up to over here? Watchin' porn or somethin'?" Corey. Pool server. Blond hair, green eyes, dark skin. Sweetheart, Marco thought, but a bit nosy.

"Hey, shhhhhhhhhh."

…experimental observations at the quantum level change our assumptions about reality as we see it…

"Sorry for breathing, Marco."

…what this all means to someone experiencing a quantum jump is that they can enter another parallel reality by closing their eyes and imagining they are accessing a kind of bridge, window, doorway to another world, with another self who has another set of characteristics, qualities, skills. With quantum jumping, one makes the leap from simply imagining oneself in an alternative reality to actually being that other self…

"Hey, Marcsy, can we pause for a sec?"

…within each one of these realities exists another possible "you" whom you can just as easily be…

Marco hit pause. "Yeah, what up, dude? You like? Great stuff, right?"

"Yeah, me likey mucho," said Ivan. "I think all that stuff is superlegit. Parallel universes and alternate realities and such." Ivan forced himself to say these lines with a straight face and convincing tone, though the truth was he neither believed in any of this *New Agey crap* nor really cared a lick about any dreamy, theoretical trends new on the scene. However, he did see a great opportunity to leverage it for his own purposes. "Hey, I have a certain matter I wanna discuss. Can we hold off for a bit on the podcast?"

The two of them gathered their stuff and bolted from the rain tarp, dashing under a still-punishing downpour and through a series of poolside puddles toward the hotel's back doors. Ivan handed Marco a large clean towel, and they both swung one around their shoulders as they passed the now-empty Rose Bar to the left and approached the lobby elevators. They checked themselves out in the floor-to-ceiling mirrors beside the elevator doors, each marveling at the plastered state of affairs atop their heads.

Up on the fourth floor, Ivan held open the door to his office and closed it behind Marco. "Have a seat, big guy. You down with a beer?"

They sat for a few minutes on opposite sides at Ivan's desk, getting dry and savoring the first few sips of a rained-out work afternoon. Ivan lay back in his chair, feet on the desk, papers and multicolored folders strewn about. Marco, seemingly still aglow from the spiritual uplift of his podcast, offered up a toast to a hard day's work. They clinked beer bottles and threw their damp towels on an empty seat next to Marco's. Marco was placing his wet socks on the arm of the seat, while Ivan was tracing the edge of a manila folder with the letters CCT in thin black ink along the tab.

"Ever play poker, Marco?"

"Yeah, as a kid now and then. Kinda fun. Plus maybe cheated at strip poker a few times."

"Ha, but I mean like in a real game—in a casino or home game for real money?"

"Can't say that I have, IP. Why, you gonna break out the pretzels, a deck of cards, and some poker chips right now? We gonna play for big stakes here in the office? Course if it's gonna be strip poker, I'm at a distinct disadvantage, what with my shoes and socks drying off to the side."

"Well to be honest, your soggy pale-ass ankles and feet are just oh so lovely, but I can't say I'm dying to see you toss off more articles of clothing. So no, but funny you should mention chips, my friend."

"Ah, so we *are* gonna play some high stakes. OK so straight beats a flush, right?"

"Nope. Flush beats a straight...and the chips I'm talking about—well, we don't exactly have 'em yet. They're being made as we speak, actually." He opened the manila folder and tapped the pointer finger from each hand on the notes typed at the top. "Interested in a making some major money, Marcsy?"

Marco sat up in his chair and looked over at the letters on the tab. "What the hell's CCT?"

A knock at the door. "Yeah, enter," shouted Ivan.

It was Nicole with a jumble of receipts stapled together. "Hey, guys. Ivan, can you just sign off on this for me?"

"Yeah, course. Here you go, Nikki dearest. See ya mañana…and stay dry."

"Thanks. Yup, mañana. See ya." Nicole walked out and closed the door again.

The air in the room was muggy and oppressive. Ivan reached over and clicked on an oscillating fan. It helped cool the air a bit, but its white noise had the sound of buzzing flies. Ivan sat back down, spun the folder toward Marco, and thumbed it over softly in his direction.

"All right," said Ivan, "I don't wanna get you too excited right out of the gate, because you might not wanna even get involved. It's a bit risky. And totally up to you. But I remember you telling me when we first met that you did some sports betting years back, and you were a risk taker by nature. That's good. I mean it's a great quality…and I too…OK, so here's the thing…"

He then launched into podcast sales mode, knowing full well he was about to hook this still soggy fish across from him. "I feel like I've gotten to know you pretty well. I know you hustle your ass off at the pool, you've got that burn to make money and all, and I'm guessing after listening to your podcasts that you're all jazzed up, thinking about this alternate reality for yourself." Ivan felt an inner twinge every time he heard himself say that New Agey crap out loud.

"Maybe where *you're* the baller sitting out there in one of those white padded lounge chairs…where *you're* the one these hot server chicks are running around for, popping champagne corks and refilling your ice bucket…" He made sure to keep a slow and steady tempo while painting the picture he needed Marco to fully see. "…Where *you're* the one with the yellow Ferrari 360 Modena parked out front with valet. Ya feel me? Hey, this is Miami—tough for us have-nots not to envy the have-lots-ofs. I'm guessing there are some parallel universes where you're not serving drinks, correct? Where you're the same you, but, I dunno…like your guy says, just a better version."

"Well. Well. Well." Marco's face showed he was pretty impressed by how much Ivan took from the podcast. "Look at who my little quantum jumping discussion caught in its web. I wasn't entirely sure you were even *listening*…thought you were just busy sneaking looks at our staff in their wet white T-shirts."

"Hey, gimme a little more credit, huh? I was looking *and* listening, obviously. I mean, I *am* capable of doing two things at once, you know."

"That's certainly debatable. But yeah, continue. You've got my attention. Interesting pitch so far. Obviously this isn't necessarily my ideal reality—you are correct, sir. Despite, that is, working for the absolute coolest manager on the planet and looking at tits all day."

"A proper amount of ass-kissing always gets you ahead in life. Just don't talk about my tits like that." They shared a laugh.

Ivan produced a deck of cards out of a drawer, slid the deck from the package, and shuffled with the flair of someone who had done it many times before. He dealt two cards to each of them and held the remaining cards in his left hand.

"So, Marcsy, two pair beats one pair, three of a kind or trips beats two pair. Straight wins over three of a kind. Flush beats that. Quads, or four of a kind, tops that. Then straight flush. Then royal flush. Players are dealt two cards...a round of betting ensues." Ivan tossed two dimes and three pennies in the center of the table between them. "This is *preflop* action. You—or whoever the next player is—can call, raise, or fold. The *flop* comes out." Ivan placed three upturned cards on the table. "Another round of betting." He threw more change in the middle. "Then the *turn*. I'm out of change, but you get the idea. A round of betting. Then the *river*. Another round. That's no-limit hold 'em. Simple. Follow so far, yes?"

"Yeah, I think I pretty much knew all that," said Marco. "I'm with you."

Ivan slammed his cards faceup on the table and then peeked behind Marco's cards, scooping all the change back toward him with a smirk. "And then, if you win the pot, like I just did, you should yell across the table: *Ship iiiiiiit!* Nah, actually, you shouldn't really do that. Bad etiquette. But where were we? Ah, yes...chips." Ivan reached down in his front pocket and flashed a pack of spearmint Trident gum. "Here's our chips: this is worth one dollar, these are one hundred dollars, these are a thousand bucks, and so on. Here's one for clean minty breath—catch. OK. But so, every casino and house game uses specialized chips. Made of certain materials, special markings or designs, weight differentials, and so on." He pointed to the tab. "CCT—stands for Chip Counterfeiting Thing. Not a technical term. Just what I scribbled down. You see, Marco, buddy, I too have a parallel universe I'd like to cross over to. What'd the guy say? A handshake or bridge over to another? This is a finely detailed plan, you see. One that can be the magical handshake for both of us. Let's take a walk to the lobby."

———

Nate and Teresa were already seated at a table on the empty patio, a few short steps up from the pool. The rain, lighter now, still thrummed steadily on the various surfaces of concrete, tile, plastic, and on the large polyester or acrylic umbrella tops that overhung and shielded the patio tables, generally from scalding sun, but on this day autumn rainfall. Windblown drops drumming on the mushroomy tops sounded like the fuzzy crackle from an off-air TV station. The table was a four top, its two empty chairs awaiting Ivan and Marco's arrival. The rest of the patio area and other tables—usually jammed by now—apparently held little appeal on this soggy day.

"Hey, guys, welcome to South Beach paradise. Another early afternoon at the Delano pool, cash or credit accepted, bathing suit tops entirely optional." Ivan held his arms open to the rain-soaked panorama in an overly grand mock gesture, as if he were a smiling Willy Wonka at the gates of the chocolate factory. He slid over to cheek kiss Teresa, shake Nate's hand, and round out the introductions.

"Marco—Nate and Teresa. Teresa and Nate, this is Marco, my top guy down here at the pool. Who, for some reason I can't explain, appears to take and serve the orders of our female patrons a bit more briskly than he does with the others. But that's neither here nor there."

"Better tippers," said Marco, extending his hand out to each of them. "Hey, pleasure to meet you guys."

"Yeah, nice to meet you too," said Nate. Something wasn't right in his gut.

"Hello, Marco," said Teresa with a sort of half smile. She felt uneasy meeting an attractive guy with Nate right there by her side. Ivan's presence, which could make anyone feel uneasy, didn't help matters.

"So! How are the new digs over in Lauderdale?" Ivan asked the couple across from him. And T, the Hard Rock treating you well, I presume?"

Ivan and Teresa had met years ago as fellow employees at Pechanga Casino in Southern California, where they soon became decent (or something in the neighborhood of decent, as Teresa might say) friends. Ivan had persuaded her to move out to South Florida, his supposed connections landing her a job at the Hard Rock Casino in Hollywood, about thirty miles north of where they were seated. Back in Cali, she didn't have to fight too hard to persuade Nate to go, as her boyfriend of now several months would've happily agreed to a winter in Siberia, had she asked in that special way of hers. Ivan had called Teresa, and she and Nate agreed to drive down that afternoon to South Beach from their newly rented apartment just off the water in Fort Lauderdale.

The four chatted amiably for the better part of twenty minutes, sipping on some hibiscus iced tea and batting back and forth the tetherball of typical get-to-know-you-better questions. How did everyone meet and when and where and so on. *Ah/nice/sweet* and other informal such words pocked the conversation. Not only were they polite responses, but also tiny fillers that granted each member of the discerning group time to peek beneath surface appearances and look for reads, however slight, on their new companions. After all, Nate was a professional poker player, Teresa a poker dealer, while Marco and Ivan drew from years of experience in the service industry, where gauging people's moods and intentions became second nature.

"Ah, that's pretty amazing, no?" Marco said, after hearing about serendipity's role that one fateful afternoon when Nate and Teresa met, sitting next to each other in a California medical marijuana clinic. "So if you, Teresa, had a more reliable supplier, or you, Nate, somehow got some actual sleep the night or two before, you two might not have ever met." Marco could tell his voice was tinged with irony, but he didn't make much of an effort to disguise it. He was trying to prompt a certain reaction. From each of them.

"No lie," Teresa replied, subconsciously rubbing her left forearm—a note Marco didn't fail to catch. She was certain that she had met Marco before somewhere, maybe in a casino or Vegas, but couldn't be sure if Marco had recognized her.

"The heavens were smiling at us that day. Mainly because we both got our papers, and oh, I guess meeting this ugly toad wasn't such a bad thing, either." She mock-elbowed Nate in the ribs, while trying to determine whether Marco had picked up on something or was just being polite in his own weird way.

Nate, after feigning injury from the rib blows, added, "Hey, all joking aside though. I didn't really care what kind of supernatural, cosmic forces were at work. I felt pretty damn lucky that day. I mean, just take a look at this specimen, right?"

While he spoke, Nate was mainly locked on Ivan, though his eyes occasionally flicked over to Marco in his periphery, as he might do at the tables to steal a read from an unsuspecting opponent. *Marco*, Nate thought, with a huff. *That stylized, overly affected disheveled look. Who's he kidding?* Nate sensed Marco subtly sizing up his girlfriend with sneaking glances. He tried to ignore it. *This was South Beach*, after all.

"Yeah, yeah," cut in Ivan. "We know you two lovebirds are gaga for each other. You wouldn't have moved out here together if you weren't. But that's not why I asked you to join us on this leaky patio. I just wanted everyone to meet. For, uh… team-building purposes." Ivan winked at the trio, as if he just told three young kids they had all met to go trick-or-treating.

"Ah, so Marco here will be joining us in our little endeavor?" asked Teresa, wishing she knew a little more about this unknown variable beforehand. *Leave it to Ivan to just spring this on me last second.*

Ivan turned abruptly toward Marco and shot him an inquisitive, though expectant, look, the sort of sly expression he might use to ask those same three imaginary kids if they even *wanted* to go trick-or-treating. Ivan was pretty certain that Marco was on the hook.

"Um, yeah, it appears such will be the case," said Marco with a slight head nod, a smile pushing out from pursed lips. "Sounds like a can't miss to me."

"Great!" said Ivan, now sliding his chair up closer to the table, reenergized with all the formalities out of the way. "I just want each of you to know that I wouldn't have included you all here in the mix if I had the slightest doubt about your trust-worthiness. God, I sound like an accountant or something. But also that this is gonna be a top-notch, truly stellar team, and the gig will all seem like child's play. A mere cakewalk, a breeze, a no-brainer."

"A berry patch, you're saying," Teresa added.

"Yes!" said Ivan. "I forgot for a second I was surrounded by poker experts—and maybe a soon-to-be expert in Marco here. Yes, my lovely, dear Teresa. A berry patch, if you will."

Pot Committed:
When a player has invested so many chips in a pot that he or she can no longer fold if raised all in

POT COMMITTED

"So why you here?"

"Some major sleep issues…can't sleep."

"Uh huh. Good one—that'll work." Teresa's wide, light-brown eyes seemed to take up half the room.

"No, really," Nate replied, pulled in like some sci-fi tractor beam to her sparkling gaze. "That's why I'm here. I don't even smoke weed."

"Yeah, me too. Never touch the stuff," said Teresa with a wink. "And those two over there also…those guys each with a pointy green leaf tatted to the back of their heads. Yup, we're all here cuz we can't sleep." She smiled a big mock smile, then clicked her eyelashes open and shut several times like a camera aperture, before allowing a real smile to melt across her face. The type of smile that crinkles up the corners of your eyes. The type you can't really fake.

Nate smiled back, certain his eye corners had crinkled too. *She's spectacular,* he thought. *Maybe, I don't know…surely, I'll have to ask her to show me the ropes…teach me how to become a card-carrying stoner…anything, really, to spend some more time getting lost in those soft brown eyes.*

<<Nate Daniels? You can head in to see the doctor now. Right through that door.>>

Nate thought about what had led him here. To this medical-marijuana clinic where he'd be pitching his story to some doctor about why he needed medical-grade weed (or whatever the hell they sold these days) to alleviate his sleep issues of God knows how many years. He wouldn't rattle off the whole story A to Z of his many years of poker playing in casinos at all ungodly hours, and those unbroken strings of late nights and early mornings stumbling out of poker rooms, and then occasionally LA nightclubs, as the sun began lighting up the eastern skies. He would just say he'd had trouble sleeping for as long as he could remember. That nothing else worked.

A friend of a friend told him not to get too caught up with the story. That it was a slam-dunk type place. That he'd get the papers, no problem. And that the modern-day weed, or edibles, or oil concentrate, or anything cannabis based, was surely the cure for all his ails. Sleeping issues included. So here he was, not having smoked recreationally since college years ago, but convinced somehow that this—whatever form "this" might take—was probably the way to go at this point.

He remembered the friend of his friend telling him the name of the clinic, which he then scribbled on some torn slip of paper. After a nine-hour poker session and then a typically horrendous night's sleep, he got up weary-eyed the next afternoon and, after a few idle hours, drove straight to the clinic, finding the place without a hitch—admittedly with fine assistance from Google Maps—and snagged a primo parking spot. Primo because it both adjoined the office building and was a quick two-lane dash over to the southbound Route 5 on-ramp, conscious as he was both that a 4:00 p.m. parking spot might be in short supply and that a postdoctoral visit might really put him squarely behind the eight ball, traffic-wise. This was Southern California, after all. He was fairly exultant at his early good fortune.

And so he found the place, shuffled through the door, and did the whole please-fill-out-this-paperwork rigamarole. *Piece-a-cake*, he recalled. Then she said—the expressionless, young robot-type girl behind the desk—for him to please have a seat in the waiting-room area.

The waiting room was like some crooked parallelogram or trapezoidal-type shape with white walls speckled with bumper-stickered slogans, most promoting the benefits of raw milk, raw butter, and, oh yes indeed, cannabis. Uncomfortable plastic chairs with intricately chromed legs lay spread out three rows deep and in semicircular fashion. They were all oriented to face the '80s-style boxy television that blared a looping discourse about some esoteric nutritional guidelines centered on raw milk and animal innards. And how cultures who enjoyed these foods from an early age had strong, broad faces and invariably perfect teeth, and how this contrasted with the thin, sunken faces and crooked teeth linked to the typical American diet. And this woman on TV kept talking and talking and going in circles, *and why, oh why again was this goddamn video blasting away in the waiting room of this clinic?*

When he first sat down, the room was empty. Then, after watching this all-too-intriguing quasi documentary, he noticed he was soon joined by some fellow passengers on this train ride to cannabis sanctum. A couple of obviously seasoned blazers, with marijuana leaves tattooed in dark green to the back of their heads. *Slightly more hard core than me*, Nate thought with an inner chuckle. To the left, by the TV, was a young white kid with seriously long dreads who hacked up an entire lung upon walking through the door, not to mention the pack of Newports he slammed unabashedly on the table next to his chair, a statement of some sort that Nate had trouble deciphering.

And there was Teresa—with those eyes and smile and smooth, unmade-up skin, and her mocha-colored hair loosely set in a bun like she didn't care how she looked before she left her apartment. Only she knew. She *had* to know. To Nate, it was a rare, captivating creature who could pull that off so successfully. And in a medical marijuana clinic, no less.

She introduced herself, and they shook hands, Nate wishing he could just grasp her warm, soft fingers for the rest of the day and not let go. But conscious of how long he may have been holding her hand, Nate let his hand slide away and asked, "Hey, maybe you wanna get together…show me how all this medical marijuana stuff is supposed to be done? Just hang out sometime, I mean."

"You sure you're up for it, sleepyhead?" She grabbed Nate's cell phone and typed in her number and name. *Teresa (hot girl)*, she put in.

"Hey, cool tat," said Nate, referencing the black-and-white form on the inside of her left forearm. "Not sure I've ever seen a panda bear tattoo. Love it."

"Thanks," replied Teresa. "Yeah, it means a lot to me." Another sparkling smile.

"Spend a lot of time in China caring for pandas, do you?"

"No, dummy, it's a symbol. One that signifies important things. Like those cannabis leaves inked in the back of their heads. Probably represents some sort of, who knows, freedom or rebelliousness. Mine means something like that to me."

This, just seconds before the <<Nate Rodgers, please come this way>> announcement from the front desk.

"Well, I'm pretty sure you'll be hearing from me soon, young lady. It's been a pleasure." Nate playfully swiped away his cell in an exaggerated motion and headed over to the front desk, where the attendant then pointed him to a nearby door.

A door by the desk opened accommodatingly, and in Nate went. The room was small and dark and a bit cluttered, *easily claustrophobic for those apt to suffer from such spatial fears*, he thought. *My guess would be that some weed might help with that.* He expected a bit more of a medical-type setting, but he didn't really care one way or the other. The doctor, *oh the glorious doctor, pure character gold!* Probably the only thing at the moment that could pull his thoughts from the image of Teresa. Not a nanosecond after the doctor opened the door for him and waved him in, Nate smelled the weight and heft of recently smoked ganja still very pungent on his breath. *All the better,* he thought. *How else does one obtain an intimate knowledge of a drug's effects?* The doc had a grayish mess of hair on top and a long, quite bushy, but all-things-considered-pretty-well-groomed beard that went halfway to the floor, or so it seemed.

Nate almost missed the doctor's first few lines directed his way, as his voice—the doc's—was really nothing more than a nonpercussive whisper at all times. A monumental struggle to pick up actual words without staring intently at his lips, Nate mused. *Fortunately for me, I've been trained from the school of self-taught French TV lip reading...so I follow ya, Doc.*

The stoned doctor took his blood pressure, offering to let him "feel free" to place an arm on the back of a chair—his version, Nate assumed, of a stern physician's directive. Then he love-tapped his knee with a reflex mallet and whispered out a few suggestions and comments about what Nate could expect, be on guard for. He capably explained the difference between a couple of product options, kindly distinguishing between "psychoactive" and "nonpsychoactive" forms and their effects, as he and Nate both agreed the "non" version might perfectly suit his needs in the sleep department.

And then, *voila*!

Nate walked out; the young automaton desk clerk took his sixty bucks, stamped his sheet, and bid him a good day. He flashed a glance toward the waiting room but then thought better than to break the spell of the perfect way things had ended earlier. As he walked out the door, he felt himself glowing from his easy new initiation into the ranks of the medical marijuana club and his having seemingly met the girl of his dreams to guide him on his way.

Starting his car, Nate thought of what the doctor had said just moments ago, about possible reactions and effects to a psychoactive substance. Nate had no idea those effects could flow from the mere suggestive smile and light touch of a particular female as well. *Teresa's already proving to be the psychoactive version*, he thought. *I feel like I'm somehow actually high.*

Dealer's Choice:
A rule that permits the dealer to name which poker game is to be played that hand

DEALER'S CHOICE

There's a two-and-a-half-mile stretch of road in France that famously disappears twice a day, the road literally vanishing underwater at high tide. Le Passage du Gois. Lovely name I first came across online some years ago, while dreaming of places on the other side of the globe to escape to, maybe start a new life, unscarred and unburdened by events. Somewhere in Europe, maybe: France/Spain/Italy/Portugal—they all sounded like perfect fresh-start places.

One semicomical suggestion said to "pack an inflatable boat for driving the 4.3 kilometer road, because just say for some strange reason you mix up the tide times—like vehicles in the past—you might disappear beneath the salty brine." *Ha!* I thought—*disappear beneath the salty brine. If only it were that easy.* For a dark time about ten years ago, that's all I really wanted to do. Disappear.

But there was more to Le Passage du Gois than that. Connecting the island of Nourmourtier to the Beauvoire-sur-mer—the names were not of great importance to me, nor that it was located in France. After the incident, desperate for a new beginning, I imagined being there, transported somehow, gazing at the seemingly clear, unobstructed road just ahead.

And I know somehow that this road is not just a road, but my life's path unfurled before me, and it appears during the ebbing tide, as if miraculously from the sea—a gift, a restart—only then to vanish again as if in a dream, or some terrifying Salvador Dalí painting that's come alive. In another vision, I find myself halfway across—sometimes behind the wheel, sometimes on foot—as the tide creeps up, and I'm left stranded, the road having vanished beneath me.

I was born Teresa Reynolds, January 13, 1990. It's who I've always been, but not necessarily who I've become.

Nine or so years have passed since my online stumble across that dreamlike road, and in that span, I believe I've found a certain clarity that seemed so elusive back then. I know where I need to be headed—my life's course, if you will—and I can envision events clearly and feel the pull of inevitability (or fate or destiny) like a strong undertow I've resisted up until now. I've sensed lately that things were changing for me; that perhaps the still young Ms. Reynolds had turned an important corner somehow. As a child, my only dream was to become a famous actress. That dream was derailed some years ago, and so I've tried to shift my focus. Now I see myself as Midnight: the center line that touches both night and a new day, both light and dark, all at once; the dividing point between the past and the future.

But right now is the present, as right now tends to be, and I'm easing into the day, poolside, outside my tiny apartment in La Jolla, California, on a Thursday afternoon.

I'm stretched out on a me-length plastic lounge chair, angled forty-five degrees from the pool, dead straight below a cloud-ringed but still skin-creeping sun. The pool's clogged with kids and parents at each end. A mild but distinct chlorine scent wafts over with each scattered breeze. Without the cooling winds to cut into the heat, the summer air would be stifling. Nearly unbreathable in its pressing humidity.

Muted sounds dance around the pool enclosure and bounce off the water and spin through the air. The whole of it gets to my ear as a muffled symphony of mindless chatter, pricked up by an occasional child shriek or wail. Though not entirely unpleasant, the ensemble.

The breeze has its own timbre to contribute. A gentle whooooooosh.

You'd think I were a joy to be around all the time. So calm and relaxed, with a cheerful disposition to boot. Tranquility personified. But, alas, such is not always the case. It's still early in the day—give me a chance to disappoint you.

I'm turned over now, reading. My elbows are propped uncomfortably at unnatural angles, injecting my shoulders with some sort of weird pain. The sun blazes down on my back and legs, gobs and dabs of sweat pooling in various places. I sprawl out a bit to relieve the searing complaints from my shoulders. The new position hurts in new places.

My mind drifts, as if carried away and held aloft by the summer breeze, and in pops Quentin Tarantino. Not him specifically, but one of my favorite scenes from *Kill Bill* (volume 2, I think), when the badass Uma Thurman character—I'm not even sure she had a name...she was just the Bride or something—gets roughed up, tossed in a coffin, and buried underground. With little air and almost no space to move, she somehow manages to free her bound hands and feet and rip through the box with repeated kung fu thrusts and then burrow her way through the deep soil, weasel-like, all the way to the surface, gasping for air when she reaches it. God, I get chills just thinking about it.

A flashback shows us how she's capable of such an astounding, physics-defying feat, as we bear entertaining witness to the grueling training regimen she willingly accedes to—insists on, actually—and ultimately suffers through.

Then, above ground, she's a woman possessed. Filthy beyond measure, and dehydrated, but possessed. A woman ready to impose her will and exact revenge on all those who've wronged her.

A compelling inspiration, if I may say so.

I'm back at the pool. My pancake flip on the towel-backed lounge chair has Tinder-swiped my entire view. Now I'm staring at the horizon, and it's an eerily sharp, dark blue or maybe admiral blue, on the same level plane as my eye view. Cottony, bottom-darkened puffs of clouds sit just above the horizon. From my vantage, they're a mere inch above the line. The thin strip of flat, late-afternoon ocean is factually several blocks from where I lie, a scattering of condos and traffic intersections stretched in between.

For a few moments, I'm eight years old again...

...the pen I'm holding is the same size as three entire buildings. A white sailboat and the pen tip are of equal size. With the flick of my thumb and middle finger, I could cause Godzilla-like damage to everything around me. Or maybe I'm actually on the sailboat, another me—*my double*—shooting a scene with my famous costar, a romantic scene maybe, the Oscar-winning director nuzzled up close to both of us with his handheld camera. From the lounge chair, the other me wrinkles the surface of the ocean with a French manicured finger to give some needed bounce to the water in the scene. That same me then smudges out the sun for added dramatic effect. The director's camera is a bit too close now, and my double would like him to back away. Maybe if lounge chair me just flicked my pen at his ear, he'd get the hint. The gathering crowd at the shoreline watches Teresa Reynolds, star actress, in hypnotic delight. From this chair, I can literally reach out and scoop them all up in my hand if I wanted.

A close consideration of semantics and physics tells me differently. *Oh, whoops!* I must be twenty-six again.

A cooing dove wrests my attention with its repeated song phrases. The air is then pierced with distant sirens from a seeming parade of twirly-light vehicles speeding off to an emergency of one sort or another. Too early for a bar fight, I think. Heatstroke somewhere nearby could make sense. My late start keeps tapping on the hood of my awareness, an annoying reminder that I should go inside and do some restorative yoga and get on with the day. And so I shall and so I shall and so I shall.

———

The daily trip to the casino. Or nightly, to be more specific. I'm generally sleeping late and then, as you're aware, often lounging at the pool or sometimes on the beach, reading or writing during the day. Plus I work nights. So…the nightly trip, brushed by summery dusk and fueled by a shaky hope that my shift at the casino will seem like it begins and ends before I can say, *Hey, pass that gorgeous spliff this way, fella.*

The routine has turned hypnotic in its dullness. Or *had* already turned years ago. Repetitive. Soul-crunching. Effortless, too, at least—*thank God*—captained by neuron clusters in some part of my brain that I've trained to just switch over to autopilot so I can get to and from work without thinking. Not to mention *through* work.

You're probably thinking (and you'd be right) that there's not too much excitement in the average day of an average poker dealer. Especially over the span of eight or so monotonous years. Of course, my hot new relationship with Nate has chased off any average days like roman candles shot at a branch full of yappy birds. And oh, by the way, *I'm not the average anything*, dealer or otherwise. But I'm guessing you've sensed that already.

This is me—the one and only, the fantastic me—now high and waxing poetic or philosophical or whatever, whining a bit about work. It's just what I do, now and often delightfully bathed in the essence of marijuana…

My cell buzzes.

"You off to Borona, baby doll?" Ally, my best friend.

"All lit up and on my way, Allycat. You stopping in? Should be busy, lotsa rich types tossing money around."

"Not sure yet, T. If I'm feeling up to it, definitely. Would love to see you though. Anyway, have a good shift, k? Miss you."

"K, thanks. You too. Muah."

She misses me and I her because of Nate. The last few months she's gotten squeezed out by Nate's and my new, over-powering lust for each other. I love Ally, but she's gonna have to wait.

I, too, have been waiting. *Waiting* for certain things to happen. *Waiting* for Nate to come into my life. *Waiting* to save enough money to move out of California and put some physical distance from certain memories here—maybe some-place by the water on the East Coast, like Florida, where Ivan says he can easily get me a dealer spot in a top casino. *Waiting* for the fucking elevator on the seventh floor to come, so I can get on at least with this evening already. I know it's probably only been about a minute or so, but it feels like two weeks longer than forever. Like I'm standing midway on the flooded Passage du Gois, stranded, waiting for the tide to ebb, time itself mocking me. And all I can do is just wait and wait for the things I truly want to happen to happen. That I *need* to happen. And I don't just mean the prompt arrival of elevators.

What's the rush, right, Teresa honey? Well for now, I have a shift that I have to start so that I can quickly get it over with and drive my ass back home. And on top of that, I have hopes and dreams and important goals that extend well beyond the all-too-cozy confines of poker rooms and casino floors. But more on that some other time.

And so what if I get high. I'm high now, sure, but entirely functional. Hyperfunctional, most would say. I clock in and deal cards like a fucking well-tuned machine. Smoking just kinda dulls the edges of things, *juuuuuuust* enough. Like floor managers telling me things they think I need to hear. Or lame-o guys who couldn't ring my bell with a sledgehammer, commenting on my eyes or my pretty smile. Plus maybe there's a specific memory or two I'd rather be fuzzy on.

The elevator door slides open, and I'm forced to wait again for what feels like two whole lifetimes, as mechanisms whirl and twist and lock and push open the wide gray doors that lead into the garage. *Absolutely ridiculous door unit, this thing, stoned or otherwise*—a big, clunky, antiquated, rectangular metal box nested atop the door's frame, with molasses-slow sensors that prompt the clunky box into what seems to me like an unnecessarily complex yoga pose of bending limbs and arching neck. *Not exactly high-tech, people.* Why this building can't just invest in a normal, modern-technology door, I can only imagine. But as it is, several times a day, the sensors pick me up (eventually) and the high-perched yoga box downward-dogs to *oh so graciously* let me pass from the platform of the third floor to the musty, humid garage bowels...

...my mind breaks away, and I picture Nate the first time I met him, sitting in the clinic next to me, looking a bit unnerved. Excited, no doubt, but unnerved. Likely from my obvious flirting, perhaps. Or maybe by just me. The prospect of chatting with Dr. Stonedimsostonedallthetime wasn't what made him nervous. It was me. It wasn't accidental. I know how I looked.

My hair was up in a loose bun, and I had on a flowy white shirt that slipped down off one shoulder, my black bra strap pointing down to just a hint of cleavage. Just enough to kick on the hormone switch from any red-blooded male, but not so much to make me seem desperate or sleazy. Anyway, I obviously had him under my spell. Even his pheromones told me.

Trust me, I'm not blind to my effect on people. Over time, a girl learns what works and what doesn't. Just like Ivan thinks he's impervious to my charms and that he's got a certain power or dominion over me. *He's not, and he doesn't. I know what I'm doing.*

But back here in reality, in the here and now, I find that I am *still* in the apartment building where I live, wasting time, pressing buttons, and swiping key-chained elevator fobs. Not that I have the first clue or slightest inkling as to what the fuck a fob is, but the front desk gave me one last month, and it tumbles annoyingly in clicks and clinks in my pocket, each and every day. I picture the up-and-down movement of the elevators and the side-to-side motion of the fob across the sensors. Up. Down. Left. Right. A cross. Am I bracketing the start and end of my days with some sort of weird prayer gesture? Am I that desperate? Oh the joy of life's little in-between moments...

(You think Uma as the Bride would've patiently waited for elevators and doors, humming herself a little ditty while reflecting on idyllic visions like frolicking through an open field of flowers, sunshine on her face, wind in her hair?)

Or maybe tonight I'll be Clarice Starling from *Silence of the Lambs*, the brilliant FBI agent who must outwit the imprisoned madman to gain information crucial to resolving a kidnapping in progress. Or Sarah Connor in *The Terminator* who transforms from vulnerable female into hardened warrior, ready to take control of her own destiny. Such powerful, intelligent women, hell-bent on whatever they're each after. Sounds to me like the new Teresa Reynolds.

These days, I get to choose my own personal roles from so many iconic figures, and not just from the silver screen, mind you. Often, I'll sprinkle in some literary oldies, maybe a bit of Jane Eyre or Hester Prynne. But perhaps with events taking shape as they are, along with my current theatrical mood, a heroine from Shakespeare might be a better fit. *You've been generous with your bounty, dear William*—so many great strong female protagonists to choose from. Where should I start this evening? Shall I play Lady Macbeth, who exercises her power over her husband and encourages him to do certain things while taunting him and his lack of courage? It's not a perfect match, I agree. We're short a husband, obviously. Though Nate can be fun to taunt…ah, perhaps Beatrice from *Much Ado About Nothing*. Such a feisty, independent woman of high intelligence and cunning, who is not to be messed with, and is even seen by everyone around her as such. What lovely qualities you possess, Beatrice. Like your contempt for men. Disdain for marriage. Desire for revenge. Even when you finally decide to couple up with Benedick, reverting to a somewhat traditional female role, you still maintain your decided edge. Kudos to you. And to you and your future portrayals, Ms. Reynolds.

Hmm…I just had a thought. What about Rosalind from *Twelfth Night*…no wait, that's Viola from *Twelfth Night* and Rosalind from *As You Like It*—I used to know all these by heart. Good choices, certainly. But then maybe I'll add a dash of Hermia from *Midsummer Night's Dream*—such a logical, calm woman who courageously runs away with her lover. Such strength and determination to control her own destiny—*that's* what speaks to me most eloquently. (OK, so I admit I might have some work to do on the "calm" part.)

Over the years, dismayed, bound up in my quiet, lonely sanctuary of a room, healing from certain emotional and psychological wounds, I've had time to savor all these and other timeless tales featuring extraordinary women. And little by little, day by day, I've let a small part of each of them seep into me, trickle down to my core, imbuing me with their strengths, their spirit-endowing, life-affirming qualities. It is this type of woman—an amalgam of all these special characters—that I have strived to become.

I'm *finally* on the smooth and stained concrete garage floor and, with images of Nate filling my brain—*some might even surprise you*—I feel my mood brighten as I head over to my car. I skip over the parking spot dividers and treat the task like a mini-Olympic hurtling event, all en route to my olive-green Fiat, who's slumbering until I wake her. Occasionally, I find the childlike inspiration (perhaps, like now, cannabis-aided) to leap from slab to slab, though their wide spacing makes it difficult. Plus, I don't particularly feel like falling on my face at the moment. Tonight, I just zigzag with shifty, darting action like I'm a champion speed skater, until I view my baby Fiat's insect eyes, and I pistol twirl the electronic car keys out of my pocket and release the driver's side door lock.

Sometimes I'm playful when stoned. So sue me.

I sidle in and adjust, strapping myself in without a thought. Then I shatter all laws of physics by simultaneously starting the car, ripping open the windows and slamming on the AC. It's a special talent. I also make sure to quickly twist counterclockwise the stereo's volume dial. A precautionary measure, in case I left it blasting last trip; all in all, a series of well-executed acts surely to be passed down genetically if I were ever to create any progeny. *Doubtful, I think.* I jam back the reverse gear, describe a sharp curve back, and then twist an opposing curve, picturing in my mind the perfect calligraphic V I've just limned, as I shoot out toward the down-sloped exit ramp, ready to trace new letters with my trusty Fiat's rubbery pen tips.

This is what routine looks like. A stupefying dullness in which time oozes by like a melting Dalí clock. Until the real life stuff happens. The good stuff. Nate is, and will be, part of the good stuff. A change of venue will be part too. Nate by my side + a cozy spot on the Atlantic + a few other things falling my way = a happy Teresa.

But right now I'm en route to work. Right now I'm a semi-irritated though trying-my-absolute-best-to-be calm Teresa.

I'm tuned into the Nine Inch Nails station on Pandora on my iPhone. Since Ally showed me how to sync it up with my car stereo, it's been loud music cranking away, with my unneeded stringy white headphones balled up in the cup dispenser. Loud, dark music of late. To match me and my devious mood, I'm guessing. But not today. Today I will opt for a lighter ambient mood. Today Fiona Apple will serenade me, inspire me with her emotive ballads. And...so...PLAY.

Be kind to me,
Or treat me mean,
I'll make the most of it,
I'm an extraordinary machine...

I'm on the highway. I think of Nate during the trip. Think in like daydreamy thoughts. Of him texting me that very same day we met. Of us meeting outside the dispensary a few hours later with our fresh legal papers. Of us going in together. Of his utter confusion about anything marijuana related and of my reveling in every second of his complete unease with it. I just thought it was amusing to watch him, his chiseled face, loose sweep of light-brown hair, and his full lips, all screwy as he looked at all the glass swing-top containers before him. All that kind bud. I picture us leaving together with our little baggies full of naughty goodies. Of us going to his place and him pressing me against the wall. And then somehow making it over to the couch and luxuriating in our own shared pool of sweat. Then I think of us huddled together on a warm beach the day after, where the foamy surf kisses the sand. Of us nibbling on some edibles during a slow walk home from a day at the art exhibit, and then stripping off our clothes and having passionate, sweaty sex all night. Some chilled Don Julio tequila and artisanal dark chocolate for dessert.

We only just got together a couple weeks ago. But that's the way it's been every day, like we have some sort of hot animal attraction and insatiable hunger we can't deny. For him, I know it's infatuation; for me, it's little more complex—I'm not sure I even completely understand it. Filling a certain void maybe, while affirming our special, undeniable connection. If that even makes sense. But it will. I promise. Anyway, so we've already fucked like six times in the last couple of days. He texted a little while ago and said he'd be coming over again tonight, after my shift.

"What if I'm busy?" I text back.

"Then I'll have to rip your clothes off and do bad things to you some other day, I guess."

"OK. Not busy. Be here at three. xo"

Nate doesn't know about the CCT—awful acronym, Ivan, but I'll use it for brevity's sake. Nate doesn't know about a lot of things. Right now, Nate doesn't need to know. Ivan wants me to involve him, says he'd be perfect, but it's not up to Ivan. It's up to me, and I think it's better if Nate's in the dark about it until I decide otherwise. Sure, Nate's pretty great and all, but if I feel at any time that I need to use him or leverage him as a pawn in some higher endgame (and who knows, I just might), then so be it. I'm not an evil person by nature, just eminently practical. If it suits my needs—physically, emotionally, psychologically, financially—then who am I to get in the way of my own long-term well-being and satisfaction? Go ahead; ask those Shakespearian women the same question.

I've known Ivan since *God knows when*, and my trust with him still only extends as far as I can spit. He's got the stink of shadiness and an aura of bad intentions. Always has. For the chip gig he's told me about, I trust him though. Just enough, at least. Or maybe trust is the wrong word when it applies to Ivan. Maybe it's better to explain him as someone face-to-face with a fierce female dog he invited into his house to safeguard something of deep interest. The dog doesn't trust Ivan *per se*, but she trusts in his sense of self-preservation. That he's not stupid enough to tempt his own fate by dragging her out by the collar or kicking her to the curb when he decides she's no longer needed. Not without feeding her first. Making her happy. Then she'll leave tail-waggingly on her own. In other words, he knows better than to offer to bring me in, only to then suddenly fuck me on something like that. I'd have to assume. Or we'll say instead, he *should* know better. I'd be a key piece to the whole thing working out as planned. Not to mention my sharp fangs. And he knows this. Except my innocent little Nathan. He doesn't need to know, not until and unless I decide he does. And right now, I've decided he doesn't. Just not yet. Not until I can envision beforehand how all the pretty little pieces will neatly fit together.

And now, *finally, finally!* After *years* and *decades* and *centuries* of driving, I pull up into the employee parking area of Borona Casino. Let the fun and games begin, people!

As I say *ta ta* to my Fiat and make my way from the lot to the elevator, I savor the last few seconds of clean, untouched summer-evening air pressing down on me. Then it's gone—*poof!*—as I enter a series of jarringly different, often harsh,

ERIC RABIN

indoor climes. Near the elevator platform, some strange, musty mix of humid air, human scent, and other unidentifiable, lingering aromas.

Speakered music blares out from different angles. Posters trumpet the coming of various celebrities and other performing artists. Ashy cigarette smears adorn the edges of the elevator doors. I press the button and wait a few seconds. The all-too-familiar *ding*, though this one mostly gets lost in the blend of still-streaming music overhead. The steel doors spread open, exhaling upon me all the pent-up odors a small hot steel box can muster over the course of an evening. Cigar smoke seems to be a permanent fixture of each elevator compartment, as if piped in by management to introduce to new patrons that cozy, familiar casino stink before they even touch the casino floor. (This is California where you can't smoke anywhere anymore, but here on an Indian Reservation, they can give Cali laws the middle finger.)

Some days, other patrons join and crowd in with me. These are not lucky days. The compartments are not particularly large. Tight and smoky and stuffy and hot and loud, but not large. So companion riders are not ideal. Tonight, as it turns out, has started out far from ideal. A number of elevator pals, in other words. I smile politely and close my eyes, counting down slowly from ten. The next thing I know, the box has zipped us up to the third floor. *Three. Two. One.* I ease my eyes open, as the elevator door follows my cue. Having been assaulted by music and crappy posters and human and chemical stench, the relief from stepping through the doors is, as they say, palpable.

I'm so relieved and weightless with joy, it reminds me of how I felt last night after my shift, as I counted down to *three, two, one*...and then sprang out of the elevator and answered my cell at the same time. It was Trigger, an old friend. I was floored when he told me his story about Vegas. Shocked, really, and then he told me the name involved, and any shock or surprise quickly evaporated, vanished like drops of water on desert sand. It was as if someone were to place a small box on a table and say, *here take it, pick it up.* It turns out to have some serious weight to it, and you're stunned by how heavy this little innocent box seems to be. And then, all of a sudden, this some-one adds the tiny little detail of: *oh*, there are magnets in the box attracted to the magnetic table top...and you're like, *oh*, well now it all makes perfect sense, and I'm no longer stunned.

I bump into my coworker Yvonne, and we hug it out and chat a bit about everything and nothing at all in the span of three minutes while pulled along the moving walkway on our way to the poker room. We pass posters of employees with big fat goofy grins on their faces. *Gimme a break*, I think. *Oh yeah, Robert Dunbar.* Big smile, Robbie—like he's ever that happy or cheerful, except when posing for large goofy posters. I rub a big, smooth, gold buddha belly as I glide by, so he grants me luck with everything. But for now, I'll settle for a decent night. Especially one that's over in the blink of an eye, the turn of a card. Yvonne makes me smile and laugh, and by the time I get to the poker room, I forget all the many dramas and torments swirling around in my cerebral cortex and lock into work mode.

All I can do really is wait for the ebbing tide so I can finally cross the Passage du Gois and get closer to where I need to be. All I can do is be the calm Lady Macbeth. Or maybe the Bride, determined to kung fu punch through her coffin and…oh, you get it already. Here goes nothing.

Backdoor:
A drawing hand that requires catching two cards to win, and in general, making a hand other than the one intended

BACKDOOR

It was Sam's twentieth birthday. Not quite legal to drink yet, but that's not what his fake ID said. Besides, there was some necessary celebrating to be done. With his boy, Griff. Griffin, really. And maybe Christina, if she could kick off work early enough. And it wasn't like twenty was a no-big-deal age. It was an entirely new decade, for God's sake. And no longer a Chicago teenager. The big 2–0. It sounded good on his lips.

The ID was a solid one. Superlegit. His other buddy's brother, who looked like an older Sam, gave it to him as a sort of early birthday gift. That was about two weeks ago, right before the older brother left for Mexico on vacation, Sam thought he remembered it was. Anyway, sure, the ID was expired, <<Valid until 10/06>>, but Sam had already tested it out in like three or four places since, and they waved him right in. Little neighborhood bars mostly, but still. *You gotta be confident on your twentieth birthday*, Sam thought. A whole new age bracket of girls to work from. Upper-level college girls, maybe even. *You gotta be confident.*

Thankfully, it was early winter and freezing outside. Some gusts of snow here and there, but crazy cold wind. Chicago-type cold. *Thankfully*, Sam thought, because *this* shirt was the only real club shirt he owned. His best option. But without his long thin dark trench coat his pops handed down to him a few years back, he looked too young and thin, like a giant weed with twiggy arms and legs. Plus he was still self-conscious about his left hand, and the coat's sleeves were long enough to hide it. Until, maybe, he had a few drinks and (*hope hope!*) built up the courage to take the coat off and give himself the first real test, the first psychological hurdle to clear; an attempt to reenter the living, breathing social sphere after a long four months, depressed and isolated and bathed in self-pity. This was a busy nightclub after all: an entire universe of people in their twenties and thirties put on full display. That's if he even got in. With the expired ID, he couldn't be sure. At least with his pops' coat, he looked older, more built. Griff looked midtwenties already, he was a shoo-in. And Christina, if and when she could make it, was… well, she was a chick, and they always just let chicks in. "What clubs are built on, Sammie," Griff had told him earlier. "Chris'll just slide right in, no problem." *I'll get in too*, Sam thought. *Just gotta be confident.*

The birthday gifts just kept on coming. The bouncer that night was a bald, burly dude and some old friend of Christina's sister, whom he had wanted to date since like the fifth grade. As soon as Chris sidled up to the two boys on line near the front, the bouncer flashed a big goofy grin at her and waved all three of them in, glancing at their IDs for a split second each like they were police badges he just needed to look at for show. And so they were in.

Sound-bar was the club of dreams for any typical twenty-year-old looking for a wild night out. Twenty-thousand square feet, with eight bars spread out over two levels, each with its own different music pumping out from its own set of speakers. Hip-hop here, house over there, trance way over there. State-of-the-art sound systems, Italian leather furniture, and top-flight aesthetic design, with one monster dance floor that took up half the first level. World-renowned DJs spinning hits on said dance floor. Well-dressed dudes with pockets full of cash, sipping high-end champagne and mingling and watching, as stylish girls—with their sleek outfits and perfect makeup and hair and high heels—flitted about everywhere you looked, like honeybees near a hive. All laid out in a little pocket of the Gold Coast, downtown.

Happy birthday to me, Sam thought. Griff shot over to one bar decked out in floor-to-ceiling red and ordered three vod-ka/Red Bulls from a skinny, shapely blonde who couldn't have been much older than any of them. "Keep it," Griff said to her, all casual like, slipping her two twenties, certain he looked as cool as he felt while he passed his crew their drinks.

"Whoa, hey, big shot. Get a load of this guy, Chris." Sam held out his mangled left hand in the air in front of him and motioned toward his big-shot buddy. It looked like a crazed puppet in the dim red glow of the bar. *But hey*, a *good first step*, Sam mused.

"I know, for realz," said Christina, mocking Griffin's motion from a few moments ago. "Like he owns the joint."

The three had a good laugh and then held up their glasses to toast Sam's twentieth. "To a kickass motherfuckin' great year, Sammy," Griff began the toast.

Christina joined in, "Yeah, Sam...may all your hopes and dreams come true, my dear friend."

They clinked their glasses in a raised triangle, each taking a sip. Then they all spun around to watch the scene spread out before them.

What drew Sam's attention next wasn't the wave of pretty girls that just swept past the clear glass doors of the red room. Well, not only that. The girls intrigued him for sure—how could they not? Yet Sam found himself looking at the bartender toward whom they were all gravitating. The tall, chiseled-looking guy, with dark spiky hair and scruffy cheeks, dressed in a stylish black shirt and glossy black pants. Just behind the bar opposite theirs. *That's where the real action is*, Sam thought. *Look. At. This. Fucking. Guy.*

He watched mesmerized, as the bartender slid bottles effortlessly from the well in front of him, loosely gripping the bottles' necks, and spinning them in the air with effortless grace. Then catching them with the hand opposite the throwing hand. Then vice versa. Circus juggler-like. At some point in between, Sam noticed, he managed to grab six short cocktail glasses and scoop up a perfectly level amount of ice in each. And then pump out, in quick, efficient assembly-line succession, various mixed drinks, each with its own base liquor and mixers. *Even with three good hands I couldn't do that*, Sam thought. His arms moved in blurry, *Matrix*-like fashion, with limes and straws somehow also finding smooth entry into each of the glasses. *Poetry in motion.*

But more impressive, at least to Sam, was the fact that wave upon wave of hot young females crashed upon his dark granite countertop. *An absolute chick magnet, this guy*, Sam thought. *To be him for like one night…be like the center of a hot-girl hurricane. To be tall and good looking and have all functional limbs—stop it, Sam! We said we were done with all that. Come on.* "Let's check out that bar over there," he said calmly to his crew, gesturing over to the other bar.

"Yeah, OK," Christina replied. "Why not?"

"Your night, bud. You call the shots," said Griff. "Let's do it. Tons of action over there, anyway."

They grabbed their vodka/Red Bulls from the red bar and shot over to the dark-purplish Round Bar, as they discovered it was called. The music seemed even louder, but also purer. *Better acoustics*, they shouted in agreement. Like Sam, Christina too was watching the bartender with unbroken interest. She suddenly dashed off and snaked her way through the horde, nabbing the bartender's attention somehow. Sam noticed her face was pulled up close to his turned ear. Sam and Griff swapped looks of surprise. She came back not too long after, a cat-that-ate-the-canary look spread across her face.

"Marco. That's his name. I asked him where we could get champagne service and then slid in on top of that a little, *what's your name?*—all offhandedly and whatnot, just before I came back. I dunno, for future reference or something. Definitely a major babe though. I would do him in a nano…"

"Yeah, yeah, we got it, Christina. Lovely visual, my dear, really." Griffin turned his attention to Sam, wrapping his arm around his shoulders and shouting into his ear, "Sammy, buddy, someday you and I will have hot chicks throwing themselves at us like our friend Marco here. Believe you me. This dude's probably a big loser. Like a brain the size of a pea. And an even smaller penis. You'll see, bud. *Someday you'll take his punk ass down.*"

"What the hell is that supposed to mean?" Sam asked, puzzled, but smiling. Griff's rambling was nothing if not amusing.

"I don't know, bud," answered Griff. "Just kind of came out. Work with me here."

"Oh, give it a rest, Griffin," said Christina. "Not everything in life has to be a big competition. Yes, Sammie the no-longer-teenager, will start knocking 'em down one by one. But let's also lay off the hot bartender who's gonna serve us our next round. This next one's on me, of course." She smiled and twirled around on the ball of her foot like a ballerina in love. "The night is *young!*"

———

After another couple of rounds, Christina hugged the boys good night outside the club. She went home, grabbing the first cab that pulled up curbside. Sam and Griff were glad to be done tossing down drinks and blasting their eardrums to smithereens, but Griff had another surprise in store for the two of them. They hailed the next cab they saw, and Griff rattled off to the driver an address about ten minutes south of where they were.

"It's a house game. Poker. No limit." Griff turned to see his buddy's reaction. "This guy Dave said to stop by anytime tonight. And that we can just slide into one of the few games they'll have going."

"Poker?" asked Sam. "Like for money? I won't know what the hell I'm doing, Griff."

"Nah, dummy, it's like microstakes. Tiny game. Just some guys sitting around drinking beer and having a laugh or two. He told me the buy-in's like twenty bucks. On me, lover boy. Not to worry. I figured now that you're all grown up, it's time you learned an adult trade and whatnot."

"Adult trade? You're kidding, right?" Sam looked at Griff in disbelief, and then turned to look out the window at the passing city cloaked in darkness. Outlines of buildings, houses and even other bars and clubs flashed by. *God, how different things were now than about a half year ago*, he thought. *Adult trade...ha!...what a crock.* Even speculating about a trade or career now pained him. As the taxi shot through an intersection, its engine issued some strange whirring noise in the winter cold. *Like high-speed blades slicing through flesh and bone...*

"We're gonna play some poker, Sammie, my friend, and I'm gonna teach ya. And we're gonna have fun! Let's go gamble it up, baby!"

"Excuse me, please don't shout in the car." The taxi driver didn't share Griffin's excitement and enthusiasm.

"Sorry, bud...extra tip for you. I'll just whisper."

The cab pulled up curbside to the location, and the two eardrum-rattled twenty-year-olds stumbled over to a small green door and pressed the intercom on the wall, watching the puff of their breath fill the air while they waited to get buzzed in.

"Yeah, who is it?"

"Yeah, hey, Dave, it's Griffin and Sam...here for the game?"

"Cool, come on in, guys...down the hall to the left."

The door buzzed open and the two friends stepped their way to the poker tables in full bloom. Dave walked up to meet them with a big smile and handshake, an unlit cigarette hanging from his lips' corner. "Welcome, guys. Cold enough out there for you?"

"Hey, Dave. Sam, nice to meet you," said Sam. "And thanks for letting us slide into your game here."

"Ah, no sweat, man," said Dave. "Glad to have you guys. The more the merrier. You know we're playing for like virtual pennies here, right? Just letting you know, in case you guys were like pros, looking for an easy game you could clean up."

"Davie, Davie, Davie!" said Griffin. "We're just here to splash around and keep our buzz going for a bit. Speaking of which, you got a couple of beers for me and the birthday boy here?"

"Coming up. And happy birthday—what was it—Sam, right?"

"Yup."

Dave handed each of them an ice-cold Rolling Rock. "There's two empty seats over at that table by the TV. Go grab 'em, and I'll get you some starting chips."

"Cool. Thanks, Dave," said Sam, already sensing his own sort of contact high from all the buzz and laughter and clicking of shuffled chips in the room. This was *heaven*.

The two walked over and hung their coats on the backs of their chairs, Sam folding his long trench coat in half before setting it down. The half dozen or so drinks, he noticed, had gratefully doused all self-consciousness about his hand. When Sam and his buddy were settled, they exchanged casual banter with the rest of the table. Griffin slid forty bucks from his wallet and set it on the table in front of him, with Dave swooping in to swap a couple racks of chips for the cash.

"Enjoy, guys. And good luck."

"OK, Sammie baby," said Griff, briskly rubbing his hands together, as if he were about to let his buddy in on some devious caper. "Here's a summary of what's going on:

You've got your big and small blinds right there, which are just like forced bets that get the action going. There's four rounds of betting. This is the first round, preflop, when everyone first gets their two cards. The blinds act last preflop, then when the flop comes out—the three community cards—they are the first to act. Here, watch for a second."

"What's that button mean?" asked Sammie.

"That's the dealer button, which has a huge positional advantage. You'll see what I mean after a few hands. Anyway, it— like the small and big blinds—is rotated clockwise around the table. After each hand, I mean. See how the guy with the button gets to act last after the flop? Big advantage. So then comes another card—the turn—with another round of betting. See how that guy in seat two over there just check-raised—meaning he pretended to be weak and let the other guy in seat five bet first, and then raised when it came back around to him.

Means he's probably really strong. Could be semibluffing, of course, meaning he's got a big draw, but usually it's a strong made hand. Especially in a game like this, where we're playing for like marshmallows. I know I'm just pummeling you with information, but you'll pick it up quick, I'm sure, you little genius."

Sam watched, transfixed, as on the next hand, three players limped in early position and then the under-the-gun limper three-bet, after the pot was raised. The second limper folded, the third called, and the original raiser smooth-called as well. Flummoxed, Sam didn't really have a clue yet as to what was going on and certainly wasn't computing the action in those terms, but he was mesmerized nonetheless. To him, the game had a certain rhythm and flow that had a natural appeal.

A year later, looking back at this day, he would laugh at his past ignorance, but also marvel at his early thirst to lap up all aspects of the game. With thousands of hours of playing under his belt, Sam would eventually come to analyze and dissect each table's occupants and action within a few minutes of his getting chips; to gauge each player's relative strength and weakness, his or her general tendencies, patterns, and likelihood of high-level deception. Sam knew that a player should spot, from the outset, where the table's weak spots resided. And other players you should avoid whenever possible. Sam would perform these crucial mental calculations with great speed, even disconcerting to a novice's untrained eye.

But back here on the night of his twentieth birthday, at the house game, Sam found himself having lost his first buy-in

(Griff's buy-in, really) and quickly down half the second. About an hour or so later, he started to develop a better feel for the game, managing to turn the tide. He made it back to even and noticed he was up a few bucks several hands later. Without fail, Griff would pepper him with certain relevant terms and explanations for various situations…that was, of course, when Sam himself wasn't peppering Griff with questions first.

"What was that, when the card flipped over preflop, and the dealer gave him another?"

"An e*xposed card*. It wasn't the player's fault, so he gets another."

"And you told that guy he had a dirty stack? What the hell does that mean?"

"Oh, he had a five-dollar chip accidentally mixed in with the dollar chips. A *dirty stack*."

Open-ended. Continuation bet. Dead money. Gutshot. Rabbit hunting. Crying call. Hijack seat. Runner runner. On tilt. The nuts. Sam got a lifetime's lesson in a few short hours, the terms slicing through the air and blissfully piercing his heart like a flurry of Cupid's arrows.

"Hey, Griff, when you called on the flop and then went runner runner for a flush on the river, what did you call that, again? A back flush or something?"

"Ah, no. I backdoored a flush. You can hit a backdoor straight too, if you go runner runner and make a straight on the river."

Nice, thought Sam. *Backdoor*. When you kind of just casually walk into a big hand. Or nightclub. Or friendly 2:00 a.m.

poker game. Or some other big life event. Sam certainly found himself big into metaphors these days, drawing meaning from all he could. How else could he make sense of how fate worked?

Like his left hand. He had mangled it four months back because of a regrettably bad decision and freak accident with his blender. But his hand now *meant* something. It was an obvious handicap, sure, one that sent unconscious pleas to other players to play him a little softer, back off a bit. (Until, that is, Sam mercilessly took all their chips, and then they declared war.) But it was also a major distraction—a dog whistle of sorts—though for other players, not Sam, who had learned to tune it out completely.

Poker was proving to be a blessing in that respect. To be good, he had to keep his focus on the action at the table, not think about his left hand. Sam reflected on the one time he allowed himself to lose this trained focus—one night when it paid off in spades. The night he would meet the really pretty blonde with the gold eyebrow ring. A gold hoop set against the gold of her silken locks. He didn't even *want* to focus on anything else. She had sat next to him at a poker table in Vegas. Usually, Sam's nerves at the table were steel, but her beauty was a hot cauldron in which steel melted like taffy. She was an obvious novice at the game and had asked him how he got so good at playing. Sam, glowing, forgot all about the poker action in front of him—the only time ever, really—directing all his mental energies toward impressing this girl any way he could. He thought he'd start with a stylized version of basic strategy.

"Well, actual play can be a grind," he explained, feeling her hot gaze on his face. "You might hear players talk about how they've just been grinding for eight, nine hours. With respect to playing well—it's a game of patience, really. You're dealt a random pair of cards every hand, as you know, and sheer math and statistics dictate that most card holdings will amount to, in poker speak, what we call 'garbage.' You've heard that before, right?"

"Yeah, just a little while ago, actually."

"OK, good. So winning poker tends to flow from a patient, disciplined approach to a session. Folding often, in other words. It can really be a tough grind. Fidget-causing boredom, you might say." He was starting to fear that he might be causing such boredom with her. *Add some color*, he thought. *Wow her. She seems to like you.* "Here, think of it as sitting in on a class of film and literature study."

She perked up. "Um. OK." Then a smile.

Good start. "For fifteen minutes, as you're dealt an unbroken series of mostly unplayable seven twos or jack fours, the professor stands at the lecture hall's front, droning away about historical context and the creative use of slow-panning and wide-angle lens in *Citizen Kane*. Ever seen it?"

"Uh...no. Heard of it though."

"They call it one of the all-time great flicks, but it's a bona fide snoozer. Believe me. Boring to even watch—forget about analyze. Then suddenly, you get dealt pocket aces. Now your professor shifts gears, launching into an enthusiastic breakdown of pivotal action scenes from the modern classics *True*

Romance and *Pulp Fiction*." The girl's eyes seemed to widen. "Yeah, I knew you'd probably seen those. Great, right? So now it feels as though the professor's incisive thoughts and enthusiasm are directed at you alone. You perk up in your chair and feel a sudden infusion of energy and interest. Your eyes are peeled wide and your blood starts pumping. That's kind of like poker. Just gotta be patient. Wait for scenes from the good flicks to come on." He smiled at her, triumphant.

"Wow," she said, laughing. "I guess you really do know your stuff. I'm impressed."

"Just really enjoy playing," he said, summoning one last burst of courage. "Hey, Sasha, uh...you wanna hang out sometime?"

"Love to."

From then on, there were no more nightmares or sudden sounds of whirring blades prompting him to shudder at odd times of the day. He started to feel normal again, like the Sam before the accident. The Sam who thought happy thoughts and looked forward to the future and the formless adventures that called out to him. Poker had played a key part in that revival, but it didn't hurt that he'd landed an amazing girlfriend too.

FLOP

Paint:
Face or picture cards (jack, queen, king)

PAINT

"I'm stealing this couch when you're not looking, Ivan. Just so you know who took it when it's gone." Teresa, always the jokester.

The group of six sat assembled in a loose circle around Ivan and Monica's apartment, discussing the intricacies of the chip counterfeiting operation. Ivan leaned against the polished chrome TV stand facing the group. Monica sat quietly by his side on a black cushioned barstool. Nate and Teresa were leg-brushed on the low-slung, gray Roche Bubois couch, with Val sprawled out opposite them on the chaise. Don rested comfortably in the black leather recliner. Lounge music pulsed softly from the portable Harmon/Kardon iPhone dock, which sat atop the reinforced glass shelf slotted into the TV stand. *Just in case*, was the understanding.

"No no no—listen to me," said Ivan to Nate, the exchanged pleasantries long out of the way. Ivan felt his blood start to boil. "We're not stealing their chips at gunpoint or taking some real chips and fussing around with the print or something like that. We're making our own. Exact duplicates. As in, our chips will be blended in and eased into circulation with theirs. Cleansed, laundered. Don, through his guy in Pittsburg, found this company in China that could produce exactly what we need. No questions asked. Like they give a shit anyway what we need them for or how we plan to use them. It's all untraceable. There's no paper trail, electronic or otherwise. Don's other contact in Asia knows how to ship the stuff so there'll be no trail."

"Yeah, but what about the actual chips?" asked Nate, his voice coated with several layers of concern. "I mean how can you be sure they'll be *exact* duplicates?"

Teresa shot him a *chill out* look, and glimpsed for the first time a glittering new painting afloat against the opposite wall. She made a mental note to revisit the topic.

Ivan stood straight up and raised his voice a few notches. "What'd I say, dude? Don't worry. It's all being taken care of. Every last detail." Ivan turned to Don, reclined in his chair, left leg bent over his right knee, casually tapping a pen against his left shoe. "Donnie, you know more about the chips. *Pleeeease* explain the details to these worrywarts." The fingertips of his hand pinched the inside walls of his closed eyelids, but hard, as if he was worried the eyeballs themselves might pop out.

Don cleared his throat. "Yeah, well as far as the actual chips, we took some samples down to our guy at the lab in Kendall. In no time he was able to break down all the specs for us: size, weight, composition, color, markings, gloss—everything. We're using the Hard Rock for the job because we know they're exploitable. Yeah, they got some intricate high-resolution artwork, but it's pretty easily duplicat—"

"Well sure, OK," Nate cut in, "but doesn't everybody now use like security tags or internal trackers or whatever built in? Don't most casinos use that high-tech shit? You so sure about that too?" A parboiled Ivan offered up his own *chill out* death stare.

Don continued, "Easy, bud. Like I said, we've done our homework. They don't all in fact use them. The tech is there, but it's pricey, and not necessarily the number one priority for every casino yet. Surely after we've cleaned up at the Hard Rock, it'll be standard operating procedure. But right now, Val tells us there are two medium-size spots on the Vegas strip and our spot here in Hollywood, Florida, that for sure haven't implemented the trackers yet."

Don swigged his beer and gently eased it back on the round black coaster in front of him on the glass table, trying to gauge Ivan's assessment of his explanation thus far. Some sort of bossa nova rhythm filled the wordless space. Not bad, he thought. On both counts. But eager not to push his luck, he filled the pause with a more detailed description.

"Lots of joints are starting to use ultraviolet markings and some have RFID tags embedded inside the chips. But they're expensive. They're encoded with a monetary value and other data...they can also have radio devices that broadcast secret serial numbers."

Sure that Ivan and Monica weren't watching her, Teresa snagged another casual look at the new painting.

"But then," Don added, "they would necessarily need other special equipment like RFID readers installed into the casino's computer systems to identify legit chips and detect fake ones. Not to mention networking hardware. Or the cost of the chips themselves. Costs them now about a buck and a quarter each to make their current chips. Would easily be double that for each new chip with the technology embedded inside. Not including the tech itself or the computers. The whole operation is pricey. Who knows why they haven't done it yet. Budget concerns or whatever."

"The point is," Ivan cut in, eager to put this first aspect to bed, "who gives a fuck? The Hard Rock has been considering it, from what we know, but management has been dragging their feet and haven't pulled the trigger on this tech yet, and we're gonna exploit the sons of bitches because of it. Period."

"That's two clichés back to back in the same sentence... not easy to do, Ivan." Monica's best friend for years and a frequent dinner guest of theirs, Val, got away with a little ribbing that others would not. From her perspective, *everyone needed to lighten the hell up a bit.*

"Always appreciate your contribution to the discussion, Val," Ivan shot back, stone-faced, but simmering.

"My pleasure," Val replied, smiling contentedly.

Don felt he should probably continue. "Yeah, it's all taken care of. Don't worry about the chips. Nobody'll be able to tell the difference—not even us. Well, I mean, of course we'll break them in and whatnot so they match the wear of some of the real samples we have on us now. Then the rest is up to Marco and Nate to blend them into circulation. But overall, easy peasy."

Easy peasy, my ass, thought Nate.

"Where is Marco right now, by the way?" asked Teresa, hoping this might be the perfect little misdirection. "Is he too busy with something? Like, I dunno, something more important than to be *here* with *us?*"

"He's got a shift at the Delano I couldn't sub him for," said Ivan. "Marco knows all he needs to know already. I've sat down with him for hours. We went over details about everything. He's gonna play his part like a nice little soldier. Worry not."

"Uh huh...hey, just curious, the artwork on the wall over there, Ivan. New piece, yes?" *Let's see how you respond to this little trap*, thought Teresa.

Ivan looked over briefly and then snapped his back around, as if just having scorched his retinas looking directly into a solar eclipse. "What? No. I mean, yeah, it's a...a new piece."

Pretty flustered all of a sudden, she thought. *He can't even look in that direction. That, my dear friend, Ivan, is what we in the poker community would call a tell. You just told me where you're gonna hide the money.*

Nate, eager to bring the discussion back to the job, asked, "What about blending in the fakes at the tables?" A professional poker player for years, he finally seemed a bit more at ease in the discussion of actual strategy and planning, his concern about the quality of the counterfeit chips having been temporarily allayed.

Ivan gathered himself and explained, "Um...so...yeah, as for swapping the bad ones for the good—at the casino, we're gonna have Nate and Marco buy in for deep at the big games with the real chips every day for a few days, just so everyone gets accustomed to them being there. Nate, you just play your regular style—you'll probably clean up anyway. Marco's a novice and knows not to splash around too much. He might lose a few bucks, but who cares.

"But then at some point they'll start mixing in the pink five-thousand-dollar-decoy chips and the orange one-thousand-dollar-decoys and the five-hundred-dollar purples. They'll obviously do what they can to blend those in to every pot they get a chance, taking only the real ones to the cage to cash out. If at the end of a session they've still got some fakes, they'll just put those back in their little chip pouches and mix them in again the next session. We're gonna focus on poker and not blackjack or anything else because we don't wanna tempt fate and have the casino employees handling the decoys, if we don't have to. You buy in at the blackjack table, and the dealer—who's handled a million chips before—makes change, or grabs your individual chips. Tougher to home in on at the poker table. Plus Nate and Marco can occasionally clean their batch with the chip runners—those young clueless kids, when they're all busy and rattled and shit...they won't be analyzing chip colors and markings and whatnot—what the fuck they gonna care when they're in the weeds running around making change for people?"

Monica stood up and whispered something in Ivan's ear. He nodded at her, as she sat down again on the barstool. There was a brief pause during which nobody said a word, tension slowly filling the air like carbon monoxide.

"Everyone good with drinks?" asked Ivan. "Don, another? No? OK. Next order of business."

He pushed off against the glass shelf of the TV stand, ran his hand through his hair and brushed off some imaginary substance from his left arm. Then he continued.

"Let's all be clear about something here. So there's absolutely no confusion. This is a fantastic opportunity for all of us to make some good money. But," he paused with an index finger jabbing the air, "don't even think of dragging me into the mud if shit goes south. There will be no ties to me whatsoever. I will not set foot in the Hard Rock Casino, and they will never know who I am. I will be completely insulated. I will appear clean and uninvolved in every way, while my spotless record, my job, my peers, my neighbors, shit—my community, for which I do charitable things—will all vouch for me. Not to mention that I'll be holding on to the money, which no one would ever find. So, again, if things go bad, which I can't imagine unless someone does something so stupid that I can't even comprehend right now, I'm a fucking ghost. If the casino suspects something, and you get caught, just play dumb and still don't say shit—which they wouldn't believe anyway—then you get your cut when the situation dies down. You rat me out, and I'm gone, evaporated, along of course with any chance or hope or aspiration of you ever seeing a dime of the money. Plus then I become Mr. Vigilante hunting you in your dreams. Entendido? Understood? We all clear on that? Excellent. Honor among thieves, my friends. Only way it works. Let's wrap this up for today."

The visiting four all stood up, mumbling their good-byes over the rhythmic beat of music. Then they headed out the front door, happy to clear their lungs of the noxious air they had just left behind.

Button Move:
A change of the dealer button (a small round disk) from player to player in a clockwise direction following each hand, to indicate the player who acts last on that deal

BUTTON MOVE

Monica thought that Ivan was a little too soft when they had first met. Not in any physical way, really, though once they starting dating, she did find occasions to hound him about skipping out on runs with her or avoiding the gym for weeks at a time. But her main issue with her eventual husband was that he seemed to shy away from certain kinds of conflict. Certain necessary kinds. The messy kinds, where things got done.

Her daddy, Doug, had spent years grooming his beloved only child for a life of hustle. It was the only life *he* had ever known. And for the fifteen years since Monica's mom was brutally attacked and killed—supposedly as revenge for a job Doug pulled before he went to the pen—the Bennett family was a two-unit powerhouse of father and daughter. A super-team that got things done.

Monica and Ivan had met in a busy Mexican restaurant down in South Beach six years back. Ivan was munching on some guacamole and chips, clinking beer bottles with his buddies, while Monica was a few tables over, quietly sipping salt-rimmed margaritas with her friend, Val. At one point, they struck up a conversation. Then the two tables combined into one. Ivan and Monica quickly hit it off, each noting a familiar dark edge in the eyes of the other. An altogether appealing dark edge. Before long, they decided to combine apartments like they did tables. And they never looked back.

That Monica's daddy was a former convict was a nonissue for Ivan. He himself had a few cousins and uncles who ended up behind bars for one reason or another, and it wasn't like he considered himself a saint by any measure. He'd never been arrested, sure; had a clean record too. But he and his crew knew how to pull a job to make a few bucks if they needed to. It was just that he generally liked to keep his hands clean during the actual job. Or maybe it was his conscience. He wasn't exactly sure. What he did know was that Monica was a lovable little poodle who had the capacity to turn into a slathering pit bull when called for. And a few things her daddy had arranged in the last few years called precisely for that.

"I'm just saying you need to be forceful, baby, that's all."

"Yes, Mon. I know."

Monica was brushing her hair in the bathroom mirror while talking to Ivan in the other room. She placed great faith in Ivan's abilities, but her daddy had taught her to make sure no stones were ever left unturned.

"Several things need to be abundantly clear to everyone involved: (1) that the details of the job are all squared away, and they should have nothing to worry about as far as the quality of the fake chips; (2) that you, Ivan Parker, are firmly in control of everything, your leadership role not to be questioned; and (3) that all the money will safely remain here, with us, and each of them will receive his or her due share when it's over. They'll believe the whole story, my love. You just gotta aggressively sell it."

Ivan was buttoning his shirt and getting ready to go to work at the Delano. His wife was a badass, what could he say? That Doug Bennett sure did teach this fine woman right. He got all charged up when he heard her talk in that no-nonsense manner. And *goddamn*, was she good at it. The last button was a stubborn one, and he realized it was because his mind was still lost in the details of the scheme. He got jumpy with anticipation when he thought of it—the chip scam. That he alone had come up with. That he and Monica had planned together. The mere thought of it gave him a pulse of excitement. A rush. It reminded him of something from his past. All he could do was smile. He was Ivan Parker. And he did extraordinary things. He looked out the dining room window and saw a morning sky divided into two parts, the first where the sun was already poking out its head and spreading good cheer and the other where darkening, puffy rain clouds were on a collision course to devour it. A memory drifted to the surface: him as a child playing Pac-Man, the game's ghosts, flashing white and gray, sliding across the screen in their ghoulish chase for the bright yellow chomping sunlike orb.

"Looks like rain for sure, Mon."

"You think? That sucks. And to ruin such a great hair day."

"I gotta go in regardless. Open the pool and then close it. Then sit on my ass for hours, as the sky comes tumbling down. Lovely this whole nine-to-five bullshit, huh?"

"Ah, you know it's just for show, baby doll. Like Daddy says, we gotta have a necessary front for a while. One or two more jobs, and we'll be set for a long time."

"Yeah, I know...Daddy Bennett is right. It's just tough having to fake being this nice, respectable, clean-cut guy all the time. Sick of it, already. Hustlers need a break now and then too, you know?" Ivan arranged all his papers, folders, and laptop together and tossed them in his backpack.

"Oh, and a couple more things before you go, baby." Monica popped out of the bathroom, pressing her lips together to smooth out the crimson shade she'd just applied. She sidled up to Ivan at the edge of the kitchen table, her mind in detail-oriented overdrive. "Once you rope in Marco and Nate, and they understand everything and trust you with the gig, you gotta treat them like they're irreplaceable, that you're placing a mountain of trust on their shoulders. But more than that, there can't be any indication that if things go bad, they can expose us in any way. They need to both trust and fear us with equal measure."

She squeezed in between Ivan and the table and threw her arms around his neck, pulling him up close. "And I know you know all this already, my love. It's just that sometimes I just wanna make sure our investment in people is solid, through and through." They brushed lips for a few seconds, and then Monica slowly peeled away. "Now go reel in these big fish for us and then come back home. We'll open up a nice bottle of cabernet and relax. OK?"

Ivan stood at a mock salute. "Yes, Señora Parker. I will obey your orders forthwith." He spun his heels and walked out the door, the worthy and capable husband and master schemer that he was.

Color Change:
A request to change chips from one denomination to another

COLOR CHANGE

That Conor Graham's eyelids flicked open not thirty seconds before his alarm was set to go off should have been a welcome sign. It should have signaled that today was certainly the day. That he was ready. Eager, even. Bright-eyed and, well, not quite bushy-tailed (he rarely ever was), but ready still for something extraordinary.

The problem was that he and Superstition were no longer on the best of terms. They had had a sort of falling out years ago, when seemingly unmistakable signs and once-trusted routines proved too unreliable in any predictive capacity. And so Conor had become a skeptic, choosing to just accept that his selection of either the red or gray underwear and of coffee beans from Sumatra versus Guatemala likely had little to no bearing on the day's events...that it was all, he came to admit, just an illusion of control.

Still, old habits were hard to break. When he was met on his balcony's doorstep by the lurid orange butterfly with the symmetrical pattern of black lines, when the beautiful creature danced and fluttered in erratic arcs around his head, he was tempted to pull from memory a few not-so-bland days that followed each of its visits. That this could in fact be a *true* sign, a knowing wink from kismet or some corner of the universe. But he knew better than to fall for that trap again, so he thought it best to let a cold shower relieve him of the fantasy.

Clearheaded, he then made his way to the kitchen, a faded blue robe tied tight at his waist and his thinning hair dripping a bit on the sunken wood kitchen floor. The sound of a bird's staccato chirp mingled with the rhythmic click of a skateboard on the sidewalk. He considered breakfast options. He decided on whole-wheat toast (lightly toasted), scrambled eggs, and black coffee. It was always whole-wheat toast and scrambled eggs. He almost never varied a thing, except for the coffee, whose origin used to often play a superstitious-type role in how he made certain decisions throughout the day. Since then he'd given up on his coffee being paired with certain outcomes, or offering any helpful signs. Now he just gulped it down, alongside his whole-wheat toast and scrambled eggs.

Clutching at his robe as he smoothed a thin pat of butter on his freshly sprung toast, he wondered why he never changed what he ate for breakfast. He still liked the taste enough, he thought, but then admitted inwardly that it was probably more of a comfort thing than sensory thing. He felt a warmth and protectiveness from the meal. It was as if the soft, buttery toast were like some sort of warm, lush blanket that he could rely on in the morning to protect him from the cold, hostile world. And the eggs were sun-yellowed puffs of cottony clouds on which his ever-weary psyche could float away to magical new worlds.

Then of course there was his inner battle with the electric coffeemaker. Each and every morning it issued a monotonous series of slow and steady plup, plup, plup-plup, plups that, he felt, sounded eerily like seconds ticking away and somehow mocked his static, monotonous existence. But Conor's imagination wouldn't stop there: there was also that certain sinister *hisssssss* exhaled every minute or two from the machine, like some invisible inner-dwelling snake steam-hissing its morning disapproval at him. Some days he let it get the best of him.

The original intention, formed yesterday, was to start shaking things up with a new, exciting breakfast. Not to spend one more day, not even one more *meal*, hemmed in by the thick white lines that defined his comfort zone. Well today's breakfast was now certainly out. But he cut himself a break, as bringing about major change on an empty stomach is too tough, he thought, for any mortal. He washed the plates, coffee cup, and silverware and went back to his room to get dressed.

His whole life growing up, Conor had been told how special he was. Was he though? He couldn't tell. All those grown-ups at his first few foster homes, the insincere people at social services too, and then his first adopted parents (before Conor knew them to be the abusive alcoholic couple that they were), teachers from each new school—everyone loved to chime in with their assurances of his specialness. But as his early years passed in near constant sorrow, and the balance of his life's events didn't seem to measure up to that lofty word, he wondered what had gone wrong. Did the special just fizzle out on its own, or did he become plain and average as some strange reaction from years of virtual strangers lying to him about just about everything: *you'll be safe here, this family will love you forever, you're going to really like going to this school, you'll make many good friends.* Yet even his appearance belied any special quality: a once adorably cute kid with puffy cheeks and thick, floppy hair transformed into this truly unremarkable physical presence. A study in plainness. His cheeks lost their puff, his hair thinned and receded a bit, his features were neither sharp nor rounded but just kind of there, on his face, where they should be, but unworthy of a second glance. Common. Dull.

He saw *commonness* and *dullness* as two parasitic worms that he picked up somewhere in his regrettable past, carving out little intestinal snacks from his gut, day after day. Slowly eating away at him from the inside out—devouring his inner spirit and confidence—and he lusted so greedily for the cure to these creatures that he would do almost anything to find it—to get his so-called specialness back. If he could just pull the proverbial trigger one time...

———

Back in his bedroom, the usual dark-blue suit was laid out just where he had left it the night before, on the rounded cushioned back of the bedroom chair. It depressed him, this suit. He'd worn it to work, and other dull ones like it, a million-gazillion times.

"I like your suits," Clara had mentioned to him the other day. Clara was tall and thin, with long blondish hair and features that seemed a bit too large for her smallish oval face. They stood behind the teller's station, waiting for the first few clients of the day to dribble in. "They're simple yet tasteful."

"Boring, in other words," replied Conor. "Safe and boring. You're saying I lack flair, and that my clothes, like my personality, are boring and safe and dull. Admit it—that's what you're thinking." He put on a mock sad face that prompted Clara to cackle, a pink nail-polished hand over her mouth not quite quick enough to stifle it.

He forced a smile at the thought as he slipped on the legs of his pants, turning his attention away from the patterned wrinkles on the thigh of the left leg. "I'm ignoring you today, Negativity," he said in a singsong to himself, back in his room. The top of the shoelace of his right shoe snapped off in his hand, but instead of casting a vicious glare and sarcastic barb to the heavens—*Oh what kind of sign might this be?*—he merely closed his eyes and took in a long slow breath, then reattached the top portion of the lace in a tight knot. His poise and calmness surprised him a bit. *Eh, my laces were all frayed up and ready to snap anyway*, he thought reassuringly. A half smile formed on his face. "Well, well. Just call me Mr. Positive." Then he looked at the clock, got in his car, and left for work.

Conor and his Honda Civic played stop-and-go in tight Southern California traffic for a half hour or so, but he didn't really mind. This was another chance to psychologically zone out and conjure new and imaginative ways to add some needed spice to his bland existence. New, ingenious can't-miss ways to puncture his safe, protective bubble, ones that so far he was always too anxious or fearful to actually follow through with.

He imagined punching out his boss. Getting stoned at work, maybe. The images felt good. Really good, he noted. Then he fell from the heavens and crashed back to earth. *As if I've even ever thrown a punch or smoked a joint in my life*, he thought, dejected again.

As usual, he made it to work five minutes early. "Like clockwork," he mumbled to himself while shaking his head, all too aware that his Mr. Positive persona was crumbling already. He clocked in electronically and made sure the tellers' window areas were clean and orderly. The branch manager offered up some typical morning niceties, followed by a not-brief list of tasks for Conor to complete during any open gaps before lunch.

"Hi, Con," said Alison, gliding past him. "What's new?" Alison was about his height, with dark hair, olive skin, and big beautiful walnut-hued eyes and a broad sexy smile that bracketed a cute button nose. And curves. Major curves.

"Morning, Alison." For a fleeting moment, Conor considered telling her about the early morning's shoelace incident. But he opted not to, thinking she probably meant something else. "Not much—you?"

The hours came and went without incident. Patrons filed in and out as they did each day, the money counter clicked away at regular intervals, and the typical Muzak wafted in the air above. Lunch—the wondrous midday breather that it typically was—inched closer. As for the actual lunch meal, no changes were in the works, nor were any likely forthcoming. Like in his kitchen at breakfast, he rationalized that he couldn't possibly shake up the afternoon routine on this particular day for several of what he thought to be fairly *solid* reasons:

1) He had already prepared (earlier this morning without thinking) and brought his (usual) lunch, tuna salad on a salad, and it would be nonsensical to go out for a burger and beer (oh, just one time!) or something axis-altering like that for lunch, having already prepared a perfectly good lunch that was now waiting for him patiently on the minifridge's middle shelf, toward the back.

2) He felt kind of drained from the morning's activities (if he wanted to be completely honest with himself, or even a colleague or two who had asked about his lunch plans).

3) He was trying to save money (as always, though for what ultimate end he wasn't exactly sure).

Tuna salad always made him happy. He loved the mayoed ooze coating the meaty albacore chunks, a decadent flavor that reminded him of his second, more loving and supportive, adoptive parents. When his new mom would pack his school lunchbox, and he finally felt warm with maternal love. There was this little moral snag about tuna—he was all too conscious of tuna's sharp population decline and threatened extinction, and on the one hand, this made him ache daily with remorse. On the other hand, however, it infused him with some sort of naughty sense of rebelliousness he felt too weak to deny himself.

"Yes, hi. Change, please." A patron with a hundred-dollar bill.

"Of course. Be happy to," replied Conor.

"Tuna salad on salad today, champ?" It was Dan, another teller, one with a certain surfer-like aspect. With Dan and the other tellers, it was difficult at times for Conor to distinguish between a mocking tone and just friendly early afternoon banter.

"Youuuuuuuu guessed it, pal."

Like the morning before it, the afternoon came and went without too much excitement. *Oh who was anyone kidding*, thought Conor's reproachful conscience. *This branch was nearly a perfect excitement-free vacuum every day. A monument to dullness and commonality.* He was getting all psychologically worked up again. He tried to deep-breathe himself calm. "Gooooood grief," he said to himself, but was quickly repelled by the phrase's utter banality and decided to strike up a conversation with Alison so he could get out of his head for a few minutes.

"Can I ask you something, Al? Like a personal-type question?"

"But of course, my fellow saver and depositor of all sums and denominations."

Cute, Conor thought. "Yeah, about that," he said, pausing for a moment. "Are you, like, fulfilled? With this job and your career and life and hobbies and stuff?" He felt himself blushing and considered tossing in a casual "never mind" and walking off, but gathered himself and put it another way. "I guess what I'm asking is: are you happy with everything?"

"Can't complain," responded Alison. "Ups and downs like everyone else, but I try to squeeze out my kicks and life's little pleasures whenever I can." She scrutinized Conor's face, making out what she thought might be a flicker of deep sadness. "You OK, Con? Seem a bit down in the dumps today."

"That's just it, Alison." An emotional dam broke loose inside him. "I'm not OK, and it's not just today or some dumpy mood or whatever. I'm bored. And I'm dull. And I'm bored of being dull and boring. And following the same ordinary routine day after stinking day." Conor felt himself being a bit too theatrical and took another deep breath, exhaling slowly with his eyes closed. "My life, in other words, is pretty ordinary, and I guess I'm just looking for a little advice. Ideas, even."

Alison thought for a moment, scrunching up her usually full lips. "OK, Conor. Ideas. Hmmm. What about an adventure of some sort? Like a vacation, and I know you're not exactly loose with the cash, but like a vacation that involves some sort of adventure. To break up the boring routine, I mean. Rock-climbing or white-water rafting. Or maybe it's time for a new car—something exotic and fast to get some blood pumping once and a while. OK, here's an easy one: go to a club after work, approach some girl you're attracted to, and just tell her how beautiful she looks and offer to buy her a drink. There are exciting new worlds out there. You're a pretty decent-looking guy and deserve to have some fun for yourself. Take a chance, I think, well, I mean…if you're up to it."

"Yeah, I guess those are some good ones, Al, thanks. Lemme chew on those for a bit. Sorry for being so—"

"Hey, don't worry about it," said Alison, waving him off. "It'd just be nice to see a smile on your face a bit more often, that's all, Conor."

"I know. And I appreciate it. The brainstorming and pep talk and whatnot. Thanks again. See ya tomorrow, Al." Conor waved and turned to go.

Alison waved back, "Have a good night…a fun night…a wild night, if possible."

From the corner of his eye, Conor snatched a glimpse of a tattoo on the underside of Alison's wrist as she waved. What was it, some sort of orange bird or…No! It was a butterfly! *His butterfly*! With wings aflutter and hovering all this time just below her shirt sleeve. He fought back a big goofy grin and walked out into the warm summer air toward his car.

———

Conor parked the Civic in an open corner spot, turned off the ignition, and unclicked his seat belt. Minutes passed before he even realized where he was. *The Lucky Dragon Poker Room and Casino*. He stared at the sign above painted in dragony red-and-green colored scales. For some reason, some strange impulse, he had swung the Civic onto exit 23 and made a succession of right-left-rights until pulling into this very parking lot and space. He remembered pulling out of the bank lot but little else until now. *It wasn't a fugue episode or whatever they called it*, he thought, just kind of hazy on the trip over here was all.

But here he was. Primed, somehow. *For action? Curiosity-fueled impulse…to do what?* He couldn't be sure exactly. Just that he was here and wanted to…no, no…*needed* to be here for some reason. And so here he was. Conor idly felt for his wallet in his back pant pocket and stepped out of the car with an uncharacteristic hop. "Here we go," he muttered to himself encouragingly. Though to do...*well to do what*, he still didn't know.

He was in actual fact walking toward the entrance, but to him he seemed to be floating weightlessly toward and through the sliding glass doors. He was reluctant to call it trancelike at first, but then conceded that it must be, as it certainly wasn't Conor's consciousness that was calling the shots here.

Once inside, he sidled up to an ATM machine near the entrance doors and stood frozen for a few moments, wide-eyed and catatonic with fear. The screen scrolled out brief instructions on how to withdraw money, but in essence, to Conor it read: <<Insert card and press enter to begin your extraordinary, life-altering experience.>>

Some millennial-type music piped in overhead and mingled with the rhythmic clacking of shuffled poker chips. Occasionally the air was pierced by bursts of laughter. A million little egg-shaped lightbulbs shone glinty-bright above him, nocturnal animals' eyes watching his every move. He wondered if the people around him could somehow see his heart slamming into his chest cavity from the lights. Some kind of weird x-ray effect maybe. After what seemed like an eternity, he willed his frozen limbs away from his sides and watched in slow-motion fascination as three crisp hundred-dollar bills were spat out with little clicks onto a little platform. *My own little bank teller*, he thought.

He looked at the cash in his hand. It wasn't enough. Several hundred would fall way short for this particular mission—whatever it was he was pursuing—and so he slipped his credit card from his wallet and glided on invisible skates over to the cashier's window. He stared at an older version of himself behind the glass saying, "How can I help you, sir?" Then he watched, entranced, as if from a distance, as a person who looked identical to him and even wore the exact same clothes and had the same credit card was handing the elderly man behind the Plexiglas counter the card and asking for a cash advance of $3,000. It wasn't Conor doing this, surely. This brazen act. This high-interest, money-incinerating act. Not the ultraconservative, penny-pinching bank teller who argued against a beer and a burger today, *every day*, let alone preaching to everyone he knew against being saddled with high-interest rate loans of any sort.

However now he had $3,300 in his hand. Just like that. For which he was paying an unconscionable amount in service fees and interest rates. Conor Graham paying ultrasteep service fees for an outrageously high cash advance in a casino. *Well, well,* he mused with a wry smile. *Now things are certainly getting interesting.* And from that same distanced vantage point as before, he watched himself float over to the poker desk.

Conor couldn't hear his own voice as he asked meekly if there was an open seat for the biggest poker game in the house. Only because the woman employee behind the desk nodded and said, "Yes, sweetie—why don't you head over to table six," was he even sure that he had said anything aloud at all. He zigzagged around the clutter of people milling about on the red-and-orange carpet, patterned with odd and disorienting geometric shapes, and then found table six's empty chair. He exchanged all the cash for chips of (what turned out to be) various colors and denominations. He thought only after having received them—the chips—that he might've heard the chip runner ask him how he wanted the money broken down, but he couldn't be sure. He couldn't recall answering her at all.

Here he was at a high-limit poker game, having bought in for a dollar amount that he in no way, shape, or form could possibly afford to lose. Money that essentially wasn't even his. And while losing the original $300 would have put him in a bit of a pinch this month, things were now juuuuuuust a wee touch different. He was on the hook for a service fee alone of more than twice that amount. But he was slowly waking up to the reason he came here. This was it. His chance. To brush up against the uncomfortable and the exciting and the uncommon and possibly even the extraordinary and feel all its jagged edges. He doubted he was ready for it, but here he was.

———

Time ticked by. Mostly, Conor sat and merely watched the action, his sweaty palms facedown on the quasi-leather padding that lined the table's edge. Poker was an analytical game, and he knew enough to get by, he told himself. He recalled beating his buddies out of piles of quarters in a few home games a couple of years back. But here, at this table, in this game, with the prospect of each new hand, and the all too real possibility of winning or losing thousands of dollars in any single pot alone, the warm rush of excitement from the start of each new hand dealt soon cooled to any icy fear that made him shudder with panicked visions of going broke. It was as thrilling as it was unnerving, but he felt almost paralyzed by indecision during most hands. He thought of the broken shoelace that he, as the superhero Mr. Positivity, calmly reattached. It gave him a weird sort of misplaced hope. For Conor knew he couldn't be expected to outplay these guys, and yet picking up and calling it quits now was simply unthinkable.

And so he sat. And watched. And watched some more. Players tossed in chips and flipped over cards with such an ease that it seemed as natural for them as breathing. He was sure they were all gunning for him. Him and his, what they called "dead money." Every thirty minutes or so, he found himself matched up with another player or two in a small pot, and a few (regrettably small ones) he even managed to take down. But his chip stack was progressively crumbling away, a sort of chip erosion from exposure to the unceasing waves of aggression directed at him. His overly cautious, risk-averse nature was certainly not his ally on this battleground. The overall experience so far was new and tingly, but still far from anything extraordinary. There had to be another level to it. Minutes went by like nanoseconds, hours like minutes, with the digital clock mocking him every time he looked up at it.

He found himself studying the automatic card shuffler. It was set neatly in a rectangular cutout near his end of the table. A no-frills machine always hard at work. Just a black box, really, from the outside. Inside the black box, unseen, you could sense a slight vibration as it supposedly separated the cards and slid them together again in some algorithmic pattern to achieve randomness. There was a round quarter-size red light that indicated a newly shuffled deck was under-way but not quite complete. The red light would go dark, and its green neighbor would then flick on, as if giving the dealer a green-eyed wink to lift the thin plastic lid that hinged open vertically, while a card-shaped shelf inched up from the guts of the machine, bearing fifty-two well-shuffled cards. Shuffle. Switch decks. Repeat. Shuffle. Switch decks. Repeat. Shuffling and reshuffling. All business. The devoid-of-all-fun monotony of it.

Conor couldn't help but think of his life in the ceaseless operation of that machine. A monotony of motion and sound. A programmed routine of stop at red, shuffle at green, open lid, close lid. Stop at red, shuffle at green, open lid, close lid. Wake up, eat your toast and eggs, go to work. Wake up, eat your toast and eggs, go to work. A perfect study in monoto-nous action. He saw his very life in the black box. *I am this no-frills, lightly vibrating machine*, he thought. His thoughts drifted to the image of Alison, and he pleaded with it, the image, to help him break free from the box.

Another glance at the digital clock on the wall…the digital bars to the right snapped to 7. 11:57. *11:57!* Just three min-utes to midnight! *But he promised himself* today*! The time to act was now. This hand*. He would do something so rash, so utterly brazen and antieverything he had ever done that he knew the wheels of his current dull existence would leap off the rails and onto those of a parallel universe where life was different. Uncommon. Thrilling. He decided he wouldn't even *look* at his cards. That he wouldn't even make a show of pretending that he did. And just shove all his remaining $2,930 in chips into the middle of the table in one tumbling pile of red, green, and black hard plastic circles.

As the first player tossed away his cards, Connor bit down hard, and the dealer glanced at him. He willed his arms off the table's padding and formed a sort of—he was now smiling as he noticed—*it was a sort of hand-shaped butterfly!* Thumb tips were touching, and fingers were splayed. He blew out with a gust, as if blowing out the candle of his ordinary life. And with this, his once neat chip stack was thrust into the table's center, nearly $3,000, all at risk.

The transformation was instantaneous. Adrenaline shot through him like a bullet train. He felt amazing. *Alive! Alive! Alive!* The old Connor couldn't even conceive of this moment or of the empowerment it instilled in him. Dopamine flooded his system. He felt drunk or high or both. But it wasn't just biochemical, he speculated. Nah, there was this psychospiritual element to it as well. He didn't really care; he was finished leading an ordinar—

"Sorry, misdeal…it's a misdeal." The dealer was serious. "The big blind has only one card. Misdeal—cards back, everyone. Sorry, I didn't notice. C'mon, bring 'em in. Sir, you can take back your chips."

Conor felt everyone gazing at him like the disappointed pack of hungry nocturnal animals that they were. But he no longer cared. He just politely guided his cards toward the dealer and arm-corralled back his messy chip pile, patiently collecting his chips. He then reached over to the side table and grabbed a plastic chip rack, arranging the same-colored chips into neat columns along the rack's deep grooves.

He stood up calmly with his racked chips and sauntered over to the cashier's window, where an older man whom he no longer resembled would count his chips and lay out Conor's $2,930 so he could go home.

This was all before Conor Graham became Ivan Parker. The bank job didn't last of course, that ship had long sailed. Along with the dull, dark suits and pale skin and thinning hair. Ivan Parker was a new man, maybe even a new breed of man, one who wouldn't countenance another boring fucking day at the daily grind, but also more importantly, one who wasn't afraid to take what he wanted, to pull the proverbial trigger whenever he damn well felt like it. Conor—that pathetic sap—was long gone.

He had done it legally, of course. The name change. He tried to make a show of doing everything these days within legal boundaries, by the book. But the new name meant everything. It meant he could cast off that long-despised persona who couldn't decide in a confrontation if he should run and hide behind a wall or bow down at the other person's feet; the persona whose view of the world was successively battered. First the shuttling from foster home to foster home. Then the debacle that was his first set of adoptive parents. It just went from bad to worse with each new emotional (and often physical) abuse that beset him.

There was still some time before the new Ivan Parker would meet Monica Bennett at that Mexican restaurant in

Miami. Monica, with that devious, sexy grin and take-no-prisoners attitude. It was she who would always make him feel like Conor felt at the poker table that day, pumped full of dopamine and adrenaline and whatever else. She who would help to further shape him into the true human he lusted desperately to become. She who would peel back the last few layers of shyness and timidity. That wasn't his true nature at all, he now realized. He *was* special. It was just hidden somewhere, scared and cowering like an embattled tortoise inside its shell. And she was his whisperer. Monica Bennett to him was like a giant fistful of multicolored Crayola crayons that would enliven the spaces bound within his black-and-white outlines. She would color over all the pain and chaos and nonsense of his past with Sunset Orange and Vivid Tangerine, with Canary Yellow and Shamrock and Mountain Meadow Green, Robin's Egg Blue and Royal Purple, Brilliant Rose and Razzmatazz Red. These were his true colors, his true spirit, now let loose from the world forever. Dull and Ordinary no longer existed. They were dead and buried.

And once he had a taste of that new life, he knew there was no going back. He'd rather end up behind bars or even dead than go back. After all, Conor Graham was really just another form of imprisonment or walking death. Now it was Ivan Parker's turn to savor the true possibilities of life. He could see everything clearly now. He had the template, the blueprint, and the perfect running mate. True heaven on earth was just within reach. And so what if he had to maybe break a few laws and a few arms to get there.

Floating:
Calling an opponent's postflop bet with a weak hand, in order to try to bluff on a later street

FLOATING

"So, how about this view, huh?"

"You mean the little wrinkles of ocean stretched along the horizon...and the smear of deep blue sky just above it, or me tumbling off the board headfirst into the water every three seconds?"

"Either," said Marco, smiling. "Both. I think they capture the attention equally well." Marco paddled close to Nate, flashing him a thumbs-up. "You're killing it for your first time."

"Obviously," said Nate, steadying himself from another near fall with a laugh. It was his first time paddleboarding, and despite the relatively calm and glassy conditions, he marveled to himself how much harder it actually was than it looked. "Hey, I just wanted to apologize for the comment last week. Not to mention the generally icy way I've been around you."

"Nah. Nothing to it. We're cool, bud." Marco sensed Nate's sincerity, and decided that he would make an effort to be similarly open and friendly. The main topic of discussion—the real reason Marco invited him here—was certainly about to shake Nate's good spirits. But all that could wait a bit. After all, allies and teammates were certainly stronger if they were friends as well. Plus, it was a stunning day, and who didn't love a good paddle to loosen up the muscles and get the blood flowing. "Better if we're on the same side in all this, you know?"

"Couldn't agree more," said Nate. He struggled again to maintain his balance, his arms flapping like some crazed bird.

"Close one there, guy," said Marco, stifling his own chuckle.

"Yeah, no shit, huh?" replied Nate. "I mean, I can't fall in *every single time* I turn my head, right? Anyway, just wanted to apologize and say that there's no reason why you and I can't be friends." Nate felt that they had to watch each other's backs in the casino, and keeping tabs on Ivan couldn't hurt, either. He was glad Marco had invited him out there on the water.

"Well, hey—sorry on my end too for whatever vibe I was giving off." Marco started to like this mutual sincerity thing. *Wow, were they friends already?* "By the way, what would you call that sort of wild arm flailing maneuver? Just curious."

"Oh, uh, that's my, uh, my wounded chicken dance. It's an advanced move—not sure you're ready for it yet."

"Ha-ha...not sure I'll ever be ready."

The two paddled wordlessly for a stretch, enjoying the silence and tranquility. Marco got lost in the sky. He couldn't recall a color spectrum quite like this: a gradient of dark blue along the horizon that lightened into cooler, lighter shades as they reached high up near the day's gauzy clouds. From cobalt...to cerulean...to sapphire, as Marco judged it. Or was that one royal blue? Nate's voice, sudden and unexpected, pierced the silence and almost knocked Marco out of his reverie, and off his board.

"Marco, if you don't mind me asking, what is it that makes you tick? I mean, what are you doing here in Miami, running around the Delano pool? Why agree to get involved in something like this?"

"Well...my very inquisitive new friend, those are three whoppers you just threw at me all at once. What makes me tick?" He scrolled through the list of options his brain presented, feeling for a second like a cyborg in *The Terminator*. A friendly cyborg. He went with the most generic response, one that answered all the questions. "Just looking for a better life, like anyone else. Maybe make a few more bucks so I can get out of this racket. I don't know. Start a business, invest in something. Can't say for sure."

Wish it were just that easy, new friend, thought Marco. *Just sum up, in a line or two on the spot, all my emotions and dreams and fears and desires. Just to satisfy your curiosity.* He caught himself losing ground on the whole sincerity and friendship thing and allowed for a bee sting of self-reproach. *Remember why you're here, Marco. What you're here to discuss.*

"What about poker?" asked Nate. "Think you might continue playing when all's said and done?"

"Could happen. Never know."

The midafternoon sun spilled across the loosely stretched tarp of glassy water, its rays glinting off the constellation of sparkles that floated on the surface. *Like minifireflies dancing in celebration*, thought Nate, relishing the entire experience. They had yet to discuss what was sure to alter his perception of the day's beauty, along with everything else.

Marco purposely leaned off his board and plunged into the Atlantic, slicing through the tarp that quickly repaired itself behind him. The water felt refreshing and rejuvenating in the blistering heat. He made a personal vow to always live by a large body of water. Just not Chicago again. The mere thought of that wacko climate made him shudder. He shook his hair out and said, "And you? Still feel like you made the right choice to pick up and leave your entire life behind in Cali?"

"Well...I didn't exactly just leave my life behind, bud. Teresa's a big part of my life now. And I can play poker anywhere—the action's actually even better out here. I still keep in touch with friends and family as much as I can." Nate gently placed the long black paddle along the board's length and risked turning his head again, this time looking down at Marco, still afloat in the water, his arms propped up on the board. "You ever been in love, Marco?"

He paused to consider the question. "Yeah, once or twice maybe."

"Well then you know it wasn't really much of a choice. She's everything to me."

"Yeah, I get that," said Marco, dubious. Not about Nate's affection for her. That was pretty obvious to anyone. The question to him was the nature of her affection for Nate. *How can you play poker for a living and not see what I see?* Marco thought. *Stupid question, Marco, come on. You know love can be blinding, make men do silly, stupid things. I don't know—maybe it's just not my place to say.* Another brain scroll through a new list. Another generic answer. "Happy for you guys, Nate. Really."

"Thanks, man. Appreciate it." Nate whipped his head back around to center just before another tumble. This time he sat down, his legs splayed out to both sides like some wounded insect that gave up trying to balance on its remaining two wobbly legs.

Marco was just about to broach the all-important topic of the afternoon, when Nate flung a seemingly random question his way.

"Hey, Marco—you seem like you'd be into psychology, yeah?" asked Nate.

"Into? Like do I devote my leisure time reading about it?" asked Marco.

"Yeah. Certain modern-day phenomena that would be of interest to people like you and me. I read about this stuff every day. Mornings mostly, over coffee. It fascinates me."

"I'm all ears, dude." *Issue No. 1 could still wait. No rush.*

"Ever heard of the hard-easy effect?" asked Nate.

"The hard-easy effect. Doesn't ring a bell," replied Marco. "Illuminate me."

"I read an article about it recently. Something made me think of it now. It's a sort of cognitive bias that we have in certain situations in which subjective judgments do not accurately reflect the true difficulty of a given task. What happens is, I think, we tend to overestimate the probability of success in difficult tasks and underestimate it in easy tasks. Take paddleboarding on the ocean, for example. I thought I'd be a good-enough athlete to crush this first time out. With obvious hilarious results. And then on the other end—the chip scam.

I think we probably both thought it would end up being much harder than it's turned out to be. I did, at least."

"Nate, you crack me up, guy. Lovely theory. Or effect or whatever. This just popped into your head, did it? But yeah, it's been easier than expected, I guess." *Good time for a segue...*

"Here's another one, Marco, because I know how much I'm entertaining you. But really, more than that, I'm interested in your perspective."

OK, guess not. "Shoot."

"The curse of knowledge. I like this one. It's another type of cognitive bias, but this one deals with predicting others' be-haviors...it seems people are unable to ignore the knowledge that they have, that others don't. In other words, we generally can't disregard information that we've already processed in our brains." Nate looked over to Marco, still eye level. "With me so far?"

"Continue, Professor Daniels. Please."

Nate stood up again, the wounded insect full of new re-solve, his feet kicked out along the board's edges, the paddle now plunged in the water on his left. "OK, well I have trouble when...well, if I try to predict what Ivan is ultimately going to do. After what Teresa has told me about *that fucking guy.*" Nate spat out the last few words like they were turned wine on his tongue. "I mean, I can't just unthink it. The guy's got some serious blackness folded around his heart. I'm having trouble trusting him. Despite his whole 'honor among thieves' spiel." He did his best Ivan Parker imitation, accent and all.

"I follow you," said Marco, nodding. "I have the same bias when it comes to him."

And he did, though what Marco really wanted to say to Nate was something else entirely. That this same curse of knowledge bias was affecting how he, Marco, thought about Nate and Teresa. That he couldn't just disregard his knowledge or what his senses and intuition told him about Nate's sweet little girlfriend. That she, in fact, might not be so sweet. Or trustworthy. Or something else he couldn't quite identify at the moment. But that to Marco she so clearly had some sort of hidden agenda or ulterior motive that was driving her. It was possible it was no big deal, something innocent maybe. That he was lending it too much weight. And that maybe Teresa and Nate really did just meet by happenstance in some California clinic. Though that's not what Marco's gut told him when they all first met. And still not what his gut told him now. *But that's not what you wanna hear from me, friend,* thought Marco. *You want me to help you focus on Ivan, try to uncover his motives, figure out his next move…OK, we're about to do that, but I'm telling you, it's the one sleeping in your own bed you should be keeping a closer eye on. Though my guess is you wouldn't listen to a word I said on this subject anyway. So, I'll bite my tongue. I'll be civil. I'll play the friend game. I even kind of like you, guy. I just think some of your reads are for shit.*

Marco thought he should get the original conversation back on track. *Where were they again?* he thought. *Oh yeah, cognitive bias. As good a time as any.*

"Only, Nate, mine's not a bias." He looked over at Nate and made sure he held his gaze before he continued. "Listen, dude. I'm going to tell you something now, but make sure you keep looking at me as I say it. Very important."

"Huh? Look at you? Uh…OK. Go ahead?" said Nate, a bit confused. What could be so important he had to look at him? Something about Teresa? *Was she in troub…*

"First off, our buddy Ivan has people following and watching us."

A long pause. "You're serious."

"He's got them at the casino too, while we're playing, and pretty much everywhere we go. They kind of just lurk around, keeping ghoulish tabs on us. And there's one right now—don't look, Nate…I'm not telling you so you look—but there's one right now, over by that little tiki bar back on shore. Sipping on his little beer, enjoying the sunshine…but really just there to scope us out."

"Are you fucking *serious*, dude? How do you know that?"

"I just do. Seen this guy a few times before. It's not a coincidence. Especially—now don't panic, it's just the type of paranoid guy Ivan is—but he's got us bugged too. Just found one on me earlier yesterday."

"What do you mean, *bugged*? What the…don't panic?"

"Keep facing the horizon for now. I don't wanna find out he's got another clown out there like reading our lips with binoculars or some shit."

Nate thought for a moment about why he first received this information while floating on the Atlantic Ocean. "So *that's* why we're out here on the water. They can't hear us out here."

"You got it." Marco thought he'd try to take away the sting a bit. "But gotta admit, it's pretty damn relaxing too. This whole paddleboard adventure." He laughed, and Nate shot him a look. *You're fucking kidding, right?* seemed to be the gist of it. "But yeah," Marco added. "That's why we had to have this talk here. Just to be sure. Even though it's doubtful you've got any little bugs hiding in your flip-flops or bathing suit or anything."

"I'm sorry, did you just say 'pretty damn relaxing'? Well it *was*, before you just unloaded all this nightmarish shit on me. Fuck, Marco. Fuck. Fuck. Fuck. So what does it mean, do you think?" Nate felt himself losing his cool, the same sense of powerlessness as when an errant wave toppled him off his board.

"I think it means that he wants to ensure his investment in us is protected. That we're not planning anything against him. No plots or whatever. 'Good little soldiers,' right? You've heard him say that a few times. But I think..."

"You think *he's* the one worried about plots?" Nate knew he was suddenly jumpy, but justifiably so, as far as he was concerned. "What the...I mean...bugged?"

"Nate, relax. Think about it for a second. You have to realize, that it's in Ivan's best interest that everyone comes out of this whole operation happy. Unscathed. Where no one makes any waves. No legal issues, or threats of his name being dragged into the mix. Where each one of us can go our separate ways with a nice chunk of cash. He's got no real incentive to screw us. Doesn't mean I'd let him babysit my kid if I had one. Dog even. So while he's shown us he can be devious, and clearly has trust issues of his own, I wouldn't lose sleep over it. Matter of fact, we can turn it to our advantage."

Nate closed his eyes and took a deep breath. "What, you mean like just keep playing nice and telling him what he wants to hear?"

"And here I was, thinking you weren't catching on. Yeah, at least until it's over. When we clean the rest of the chips and get our payouts."

"You're still so sure he's gonna deliver on his word, even with the freaking surveillance net he's got us in?"

"Not one hundred percent. But when can you be? My assumption is that inside his devious brain, there's some sort of war playing out, *and the fucking dominant forces of self-preservation will win out and fucking crush, like they goddamn should, the overmatched, pathetic soldiers of greed.*" Marco was trying out his own Ivan impression.

"Nice visual. Accent needs work though."

The two sat floating in silence for a few minutes, as Nate started to process what he'd just been told.

"Makes sense," said Nate. "I guess you're right. People who come up with schemes like that are just twisted by nature. Twisted and paranoid. Doesn't mean he doesn't want the whole thing to work out as planned."

"Exactly."

Marco gave Nate some more time to digest it all. He figured it might be better to keep it light for a bit. "Hey, speaking of working out, this paddleboarding is something else, huh?" asked Marco.

"Oh yeah," said Nate, happy for the distraction. "I'll be sore tomorrow in places I long forgot about."

Another long pause. "Listen," said Marco. "Just think of it for now as in the middle of big poker hand. Multiway action. Your turn to act. You've got several players at the table watching your every move, some even looking at your neck pulse, for Christ's sake. This is just like that for the time being. Just gotta keep it cool. Play your cards right. It'll pay off."

"Shit! I just realized," said Nate. "I don't know what Teresa and I may have already said about Ivan while he was listening." Nate tried to do a quick mental inventory of the last few weeks. "I guess, from here on out, I'm going to have to write everything down for Teresa. Who knows where all the bugs are?"

"Exactly. Writing's a good idea."

"Wait a second. Are they listening to us in bed? What if there's cameras and shit?"

"Well, didn't Teresa say she always wanted to be an actress?" said Marco with almost immediate regret. He knew he just earned another look from Nate. "Kidding. Just kidding. I'd say to just play the game a little while longer and then we'll make sure we get everything debugged. Then you'll have so much privacy, you won't know what to do with it. Think you might wanna wrap this up soon?"

"Just play the game, huh? *God*, this sucks!" Nate's crumpled face would have been hilarious were it under different circumstances. "I don't know who I can even trust anymore! *Ahhhh!*" After his little venting episode, Nate couldn't remember if Marco had just asked him a question or not. "What, so, you wanna head in?" asked Nate.

"Yeah." said Marco. "But, you know what? First let me pose a question to you, college boy. It'll be good practice, as we transition into Big Brother world back on shore." Marco hopped back up on the board and grabbed his paddle, peering down over his left shoulder at Nate. "Why do you think it is that guys like us are so interested in the issue of trust? Of learning how to sniff out lies or acts of deception? Of staying hypervigilant against someone in our own little worlds betraying us?"

"Uh, not sure," said Nate, considering the question. He perked up, about to mention his favorite topic. "Poker has definitely focused my attention on lying and cheating and, I guess, different forms of deception. Combine that with some experiences in my past when I've been let down, when my trust's been betrayed. Those times stick with you. Make you a bit more aware of people, maybe suspicious of their intentions sometimes."

"Exactly. Poker's probably just honed your ability to focus on it. But you've been lied to or betrayed before. Many times, I'm guessing. Who hasn't? I could tell you some shit about my past that would knock your socks off." Marco could tell by Nate's demeanor that was striking the right cord. Nate seemed to be himself again. "But what's the alternative? We can't just go through life assuming the whole world, like everyone we meet, is full of shit, right? I mean we have to expose ourselves at some point, become vulnerable. Or else what? What's the alternative? Just hide in a cave and suspect everyone out there is the enemy, plotting against us? Form no relationships or let anyone into your world? Never make new friends? Or fall in love?"

Hey, look at me really opening up to my new friend, thought Marco. *Even about falling in love. That one, though, should include some sort of corollary.*

"Aha!" said Nate. "I knew you and I were cut from the same cloth. I like how your brain works, Marco. All right, I'm trying really hard to relax and stay focused here. OK, well as I see it, it's like this beautiful sky above. All these different shades of blue, lying along a wide spectrum. We could view lying, betrayals, and deceptions falling along a similar spectrum, right?"

Marco almost couldn't believe his ears. Nate had stolen his thought. Marco chimed in, pointing to an area of lighter-blue shade, far up from the horizon. "Like a little white lie that hurts no one might fall in that area over there."

"What's that, periwinkle or something?" Nate was really enjoying the distraction now.

"Closer to sapphire, I'd say," said Marco.

"OK, and so maybe on the other end," said Nate, "there's maybe the ultimate lie or deception, the greatest of all betrayals of trust—by a close friend, trusted adviser, family friend, loved one. The type that crushes someone to the core or even affects the very course of lives. We'll put those right there along the horizon. By the royal blue."

"Pretty sure that's cobalt, bud. But I'd have to agree with your assessment. Spot-on."

Marco stared out in another reverie at the distance before him. This topic always set his mind adrift. *So how do we know when we can really trust someone? Truly. How do we know for sure we can even trust each other, Nate? Is it time itself that establishes trust? That, combined with trial by fire? Does this bonding moment solidify our mutual trust? Or maybe it just comes down to intuition and reading abilities, like in poker? Remember your early read on me, not too long ago? We haven't exactly been battle tested, nor have we known each other for any significant period of time. So what reason do we have to trust each other in any meaningful way? Most betrayals, however modest, have the surface appearance of mutual trust, don't they? Otherwise a crushing betrayal would never even take place. Almost by definition, right? After today, and our little bonding session, we'd both be pretty surprised and disappointed, crushed even, by a betrayal from the other. Maybe it just means the deeper the bond of trust, the more vulnerable you become to betrayal and the more vigilant you might need to be—not suspicious, cynical, or pessimistic—but vigilant. Just because then you have so much to lose. Gotta have faith, I guess. Listen and pay heed to your intuition and reads, while still having faith in the person, and, I don't know, in the overall goodness of humanity, maybe. That there's more good apples than bad. Kind of a weird numbers game, now that I think of it.*

"That there's more good apples than bad," Marco muttered suddenly out loud, unwittingly.

"Say what?" asked Nate, his own trance broken by Marco's non sequitur. "What's that about apples?"

"Nothing, nothing. Just the end of a thought that kinda popped out."

"Gotcha. Maybe you should get that looked at. I might know somebody." Nate sneaked a glance over to the tiki bar Marco had mentioned earlier, but it was empty. "Should we head in? I feel like we have a captive audience eagerly awaiting our return."

"Yeah, let's do it. Hey, I know what'll make you feel better. You hungry? Ever have a pitaya bowl?" asked Marco.

"A what? What's that, like an açai bowl?"

"Pitaya. Dragonfruit. Yeah, similar a bit to açai. It's perfect after a paddle. We'll grab a couple when we dry off. We can practice our 'good little soldiers' routine. It'll be great." Marco smiled, knowing that a sharp look from Nate was probably on its way.

Nate just laughed to himself instead. "Yeah, I can eat."

Twenty minutes later, seated at the cafe, a pitaya bowl in front of each of them, Nate couldn't resist: "Hey, speaking of apples, pal, this shit looks like mashed apples blended with fuchsia-colored paint. Not that I'm not excited or anything, but you sure it's edible?"

"It's a smidge tastier than paint. Though maybe slightly more toxic. Kidding. It's delicious. I promise."

I promise, thought Marco, dismissively. *What did that even mean in their world now?*

"Bon appétit. And good talk today, buddy." Marco tilted his head down and opened his eyes wide like some weird hypnotist move, but Nate correctly interpreted it as a stern reminder of what they'd discussed earlier. *Something about a bunch of people following them and bugs planted everywhere...*

"Yeah, Marco," said Nate, his voice betraying a laundry list of emotions. He shook his head again in disbelief. "Good talk."

Gutshot:
To draw to and/or hit an inside straight

GUTSHOT

These days, nostalgia could leap from the shadows at any time and get Nate all choked up. Southern Florida was OK, he guessed (and Teresa was obviously "the nuts"), but it couldn't sniff at his native California. The incomparable beauty, soothing tranquility, and near-perfect climate envied the world over. Yeah, Nate missed his lifelong home, but it wasn't just the geography of it. He missed his family (well some of his family, anyway) and the friends he'd left behind, along with the genuine delight he got from the instructional poker group he hosted—a group who came to him, sought out his skills, and paid him for his knowledge—near his grandfather's home in Escondido.

Escondido was a city in the north county of San Diego, a shallow valley ringed with rocky hills. The name itself was a source of inspiration and intrigue for many—*escondido*: hidden, in Spanish. Some said that it referred to hidden sources of water or, even better, thought Nate growing up, hidden treasure, something his tireless childhood adventures with friends had borne out time and again. They were always unearthing treasure in one form or another, be it little animal fossils, cool arrow tips, or even secret bike paths through the hills they'd thought they discovered themselves.

Hidden. Over the years though, Nate came to learn far darker connotations for the word given to his grandfather's town. As in, secrets and scandals or dark truths, either long buried in the past or lurking just beneath the surface of present-day life around him. Not his own, for sure, as the worst he could remember he'd ever done was set off firecrackers well after July Fourth had passed. For the rest of his family, especially his brother and his shadowy, checkered past, the word *escondido* and its connotation might be apt. That dark sense of the word stayed with him every time he was there, yet it wasn't until he began playing poker for a living and started a flourishing business as a group poker instructor that he truly grasped how *escondido* might aptly refer to the human condition.

Nate got an early taste of how gambling screwed with his own biochemical systems. One prime example was the disruption of sleep: it was like a five-hundred-pound sumo wrestler stiff-arming him awake, shoving him out of the ring of peaceful slumber. But that was just one example. He didn't particularly like the way poker made him *feel*, either—this, despite his passion for the game. And the way he viewed it as a truly pure form of competition. When he got lucky in a pot or played a hand with crafty genius, sure, it felt good. Like the typical glow of pride that came from analyzing a hand correctly or making the right read or decision. It was usually amplified by a pleasant jolt of dopamine, making him feel warm and fuzzy. You could see it on his face, as plain as day. On any player's face. But then on the other end of the spectrum, when he lost a big pot or, worse, session, with someone (typically an inferior player) getting lucky on him, or making a move that defied all logic and comprehension but that ultimately would win the pot off Nate—that was the worst of all feelings. Like a hard punch in the gut, that disintegrated all his internal organs all at once. Whatever biochemical process was going on there, the emptiness or hollowness was intensely unpleasant. Nate knew this well. Though to much of the outside world, it was *hidden*.

The gambling world was a strange place, he knew, along with the type of individuals drawn to it. The unsavory types who tended to thrive under the influence of alcohol or the cover of darkness. They all seemed harmless at times. But if you played enough, you might get a true glimpse of the darkness *hidden* within many of these souls. Nate certainly did.

He was back now in Escondido, his spongelike memory recalling with fine detail previous poker class sessions. One thing he came up with, as a sort of needed break between strategic discussions of hands, was to often allow his students (usually twenty per class, paying a fee of $100 per hour) to offer up their experiences and interpretations of their feelings. Or specifically, what they felt was going on inside their bodies as they played poker for stretches in casinos or home games. It certainly wasn't crucial to know the biochemical processes at work while playing, but for many, it would help them devise practical techniques or solutions for remaining calm in the heat of battle. During this scheduled break time, it always surprised Nate how most students would almost jump out of their skin, eager to contribute:

Kirk: "I'm obviously a drug guy, and I don't try too hard to hide it. (A swell of laughter filled the room.)

It's just part of my makeup. Biochemical or otherwise. I've tried just about everything over the years. Some stuff is better than others, obviously. I just smoke weed these days, so let's all just calm down. (He laughed along with the class.) But I mean, I say this because… so like I know a ton of people who get high and stuff on buckets of ice cream. Or like Hostess Cup Cakes. The sugar high and whatever. What's the difference? Drugs, sugar, gambling—it's all the same inner reward systems at work, right?"

At this, Nate pictured Teresa, wearing nothing but panties, a small marijuana pipe in her hand. He thought, *Yeah, and why don't we add deadly women with high-potency medical marijuana into the mix as well. "Psychoactive" women and marijuana.* He decided to chime in.

Nate: "Yeah, well, with poker of course, aside from strategy and analytical thought—not to get too technical—but under the surface it's all just a fun little interplay among biochemical, electrical, and neuronal circuitry…as in, signals are fired, brain particles are misted about, and you feel certain things and behave in certain ways."

Liz: "Yeah, like when your dopamine receptors go kinda nuts during a session. Like in big pots and stuff. Or if there's a ton of money on the line. And it's a crazy feeling…like when you're waiting for the flop and you hit a set, it's both the…it's the lead-up, the anticipation before it comes out and you get kinda jazzed up, and then if you flop it, you get the full dopamine buzz. Just like taking a hit of coke, is my thinking. A line or whatever.

It only lasts if you win the hand, and if you do and it's a big pot, then another little hit. Or maybe a major hit, again depending on the size of the pot and the money you've put at risk."

Nate smiled as he thought of his own lead-up and anticipation in the minutes before he would meet up with Teresa that first night. *Damn straight, those receptors go nuts.*

The sound of crunching filled the small room, as Nate too felt obligated to keep the classes as clean as possible. With respect to food and beverages, anyway. Tortilla chips, whole grain crackers, carrots, celery, humus, guacamole, iced tea, coffee. No smoking of any sort. That sort of thing. The last thing he wanted was word that his little groups were just glorified house parties where they smoked joints, drank beer, and gambled and such. The class seemed to appreciate it. *They were certainly paying for it*, he thought.

Tito: "But then, hey, if you lose a pot like that...you guys all know it—it's like you get that early jolt right and you're kinda hopped up a bit, and then let's say you get the money in and then the dude—or gal, excuse me, ladies—and then the person you're up against puts all his or her chips in on some flush draw or tries to bluff you or something and just smashes the river. Like catches the perfect card and wins the pot. Duuuuuuuude...it's like you get this pit in your gut. It's this antihigh. Let's say like you left your dog in the car with the windows rolled up on like a one-hundred-ten-degree day. And just like forgot about him. And then you realize when you're like miles away. It just hits you. It's that kind of feeling."

Scattered moans dribbled out across the room.

Liz: "Oh Tito, that's gross. Come on."

Tito: "Or like you got like eight balls spread out all across this table and then you hear the cops pounding at the front door and yelling about warrants and shit and that they're coming in. Maybe, for your quieter types, you just forgot your wife's birthday or some shit. It's like *that* feeling."

Nate let them all ramble on for a stretch, his students enjoying the camaraderie of shared experience. Or maybe it was just a chance to vent at things gnawing at them, still early in their poker endeavors. It didn't matter. Everyone seemed on board with it.

Peter: "Yeah, we can all definitely relate. That emptiness inside like you got blasted by a shotgun in the gut, and it's all hollow but kinda burning around the edges. And you start getting faint, like all your blood's seeping out. Like someone reaches into your chest and just rips out all your internal organs in one tug."

Lewis: "Yeah, Pete, and when you actually *win*—though you, of course, won't know too much about this feeling—but when you win, and you can feel all weightless and tingly and high, floating and shit…like these beautiful angels are holding you up in the clouds while you're sipping on chocolate milk shakes and shit."

Peter: "Wow, quite the poet, Lew."

Lewis: "And like bam! It can all be wiped away with a bad card or two, and like forget about floating on clouds and shit; you're all hollowed and gutted out…have trouble speaking and even breathing."

Nate: "Ha! Awesome descriptions, guys. Love it. Lemme get technical real quick. I just want to add what I have highlighted here in this book, on the circuitry of the pleasure and reward system: A spray of dopamine and/or adrenaline shoots across a space and tickles the spidery tips of the densely branched dendrites. A chemical signal jets along the axon at quantum speeds and sets off a wave of subsequent chemical activity. In nanoseconds, you feel…

…*psychoactive*, he thought to himself, knowing that was the wrong use of the word, but drawn to it again.

"Well, you feel pretty damn good, right? All right, so back to some actual card strategy," said Nate to the class. "Slowplaying—define it. Jacky."

"It's, uh…deceptive play in poker where we play weakly or passively to, uh…to disguise the strength of our hand."

"Perfect. OK and when do we wanna *slowplay*? Complex answer, I realize, and we'll go over it again in a bit with some actual hand situations. Generally when we make a huge hand and think we might scare someone off if we raise too early. On the flip side, of course, is that if you slowplay too often or at the wrong times, then you're apt to fall way short on maximizing your profits, not to mention that you might let someone with a weak hand who might have folded to a bet, instead catch up and really stick it to you. What about a *squeeze*? Vic."

"It's when you reraise after there's…after there's already been a raise and maybe someone else is in the pot too…" Vic's voice tailed off.

"Uh…close enough," said Nate. "Yeah. When there's a raise preflop and at least one caller and then you reraise. And when should we think about squeezing? When we think we can get the first player to fold, since he might be weak, plus he doesn't know what the other players behind him will do… sometimes an easy way to pick up small pots without even needing much of a hand."

"*Squeeze play*," Nate muttered to himself. *In this dark world of poker—and in the messy game of life he had come to know—someone was always looking to squeeze someone else, it seemed.* Money, drugs, scams.

And with this, his attention flicked back to word *hidden*. He thought of some of the shady things people had done over the years, and then of Ivan, the perfect embodiment of the word *shady*. Maybe even a new species. His intentions always seemed to be hidden. Perpetually shrouded in a cloak, woven through with the many threads of suspicion, deception, and distrust.

Even Marco, he thought. He remembered not long after meeting Marco on the Delano patio that rainy day, with Teresa by his side, and Ivan doing his spiel, when he couldn't believe he heard himself correctly. Off to the side, he told Marco that he was *on to him*. Marco had said something like, You're *on* to me? What the fuck does that mean? Just play your part and keep your eyes on your girlfriend or whatever, dude. *Maybe a screw up on my part*, thought Nate. But Marco was just a little too smooth with everything. Mr. Cool. Mr. Unconcerned. Mr. Innocent. Just seemed to glide about, finding his way into the discussion and not making too many waves. *Can't put my finger on it. My reads are usually solid*, he thought at the time. *But I guess I should be careful of trying to see things that aren't necessarily there. As far as Ivan goes, though, I know my read is right. That fucker is the inverse of Teresa: he's active psycho.*

Hollywood:

"Hollywood" refers to acting or talking in an exaggerated way, so as to encourage a specific reaction from an opponent during a hand. "Hollywooding" often refers to actions intended to be deceptive, such as when a player talks a great deal and acts comfortable, thus appearing very strong, when in fact the player's hand is weak.

HOLLYWOOD

The invitations to Jacky's sweet-sixteen birthday party had little pandas holding red roses. Jacky herself came up with the idea. Even her mom would back her up on that. Sure, it was her mom who designed the rest, but come on. Everyone knew it was the pandas that made the cards.

High school was a time for the popular kids to stand out and shine. Jacky was certainly one of those: a thick mane of blondish hair and delicate features set on a heart-shaped face, captain of the JV cheerleading squad, and girlfriend to one Tommy Adams—nothing special really—just a senior with drop-dead looks, the quarterback of the varsity football team, and oh, the virtual king of Stony Ridge High School. So yeah, Jacky was known to walk through the halls with a certain pronounced swagger, and could have pretty much invited the whole school to her party. But her mom said only fifty people, so that would have to do.

Obviously Teresa was invited. Her best friend and closest confidant (and probably second-most-popular sophomore girl, in Jacky's opinion), Teresa even helped her pick out the theme. They would do a Hollywood theme with a red-carpet-type event, with everyone having to dress in black and white (fake tuxedo-print shirts encouraged). Except for Jacky, who would be decked out in red to steal the show. As it should be for her sweet sixteen, Jacky thought.

Her parents rented out a little hall near the Lucky Strike bowling alley and hired a DJ and a catering company. Mini tacos and sliders and such. Plus there would be cardboard cut-outs of celebrities like Tom Cruise and Megan Fox, so that everyone could take pictures with the stars and show them off at school the next week.

Teresa said she was coming with Seth, as was expected. They had only been dating for a couple of weeks, but they were already like the second-most-popular couple, next to Jacky and Tommy obviously. But yeah, so that made four so far. The rest, Jacky thought, were lackeys and wannabes and everything in between, but they were still her *friends*, she guessed, and any-way she needed them to attend and fill out the biggest event of this high-school year.

The party kicked off to a roaring success. Jacky had sat down with the DJ earlier and told him all her favorite mu-sic. Every song he played was a hit. People in their fake tuxes and mock-glam dresses danced like there was no tomorrow, hopped up on cake and soda and pizza and candy and what-ever else they could get their teenage hands on. The cutouts looked almost lifelike and helped create some seriously rad pics. Jacky especially loved the one her mom took of her and Ryan Gosling, though Tommy said he didn't think it came out that great. *Boys*, thought Jacky, shaking her head.

At one point, Teresa, who had just been by her side on the dance floor a little while ago, seemed to vanish into thin air. And Seth too, nowhere to be found. *Aha! So that's where she probably is. Looks like someone aside from me is getting some action tonight*, she thought.

But what Jacky couldn't know was that Teresa was in the midst of what would become the single worst experience of her young life, a living nightmare that would shape her for many years to come.

Seth had pulled Teresa by the hand and led her to back to his black Nissan Pathfinder. Why, she asked. Well, so they could sneak some shots of Jack Daniels out of minibottles in the backseat. And maybe make out a bit. Up to that point, after the few weeks they'd been together, Seth, a year older and much more experienced, hadn't been given the green light to do much more than kiss, along with a bit of over-the-clothes groping. This was his opportunity to loosen up her defenses and take her the way he really wanted.

A touch of ketamine in her bottle should do the trick, Seth thought, having planned for this moment several days before. His buddy Jacob had found him the stuff, supposedly tasteless and odorless, though he didn't really explain to him how to use it. Seth wasn't sure exactly how much he should dust in the bottle to get her to relent, so he figured he'd put about twice as much as he tested on himself the day before—*about yay much*, and this way she'd either be putty in his hands or knocked out completely. He didn't really care which. As long as he could get what he wanted out of this hot little sophomore, sooner than later.

After a few minutes in the backseat, Teresa started complaining that she really didn't feel too well, and could he just stop and let her breathe, collect herself for a little bit. But she was fading quickly, and a minute or two after that, she blacked out. Seth decided it best to lay her down in the backseat, so no one passing by could see her. Then he jumped behind the wheel and sped off to his house, now empty for the evening. Once in the safety of his garage, he pulled Teresa out of the backseat and carried her to his bedroom, where he would spend the next half hour or so bypassing any and all previous red lights and ripping to shreds a young Teresa's sense of innocence, trust, control, and personal safety.

Back at the hall, the evening grew late, and Jacky grew irritated. Her best friend was gone and not responding to her texts or calls. Only then did Jacky decide that something could be wrong. She relayed her concern to Tommy, and he started to make a few calls to find out what he could. Nobody seemed to know anything.

Back at his empty house, Seth, now a bit panicky, had called his brother who had gone to see a movie. He needed him to come over *ASAP* to help him with a major problem. *Seriously, bro, come on*, he said, *I need you like right now.*

His older brother Nate texted him back that he'd be right over, and to calm down; they'd figure out whatever it was. Nate was shocked to discover his help was required because Seth's girlfriend had passed out and was unresponsive. Nate peeked in the room and saw a baseball hat tilted low on the girl's head. Then he jumped back out, as if burned. *What the fuck, Seth?*

What did you do? Not that he would ever admit to it, but his brother had put the hat on her to prevent him from having to look at the face of the person he'd just sexually assaulted and raped. Nate looked directly at his brother and noticed the cold desperation in Seth's own face. He figured he'd get all the answers he needed later, after the poor young girl in Seth's room was taken to the hospital, and it was determined she was OK. But Nate himself now felt *off* somehow, his composure gone, his face flushed, and mind encased in fog, his conscience waffling about how to handle the situation. He was trying to think through the haze...*OK, OK*...he *would* help, but he would have *as little to do* with the situation as possible, in all aspects. *That* was his decision. He didn't know *who the tramp was* and didn't wanna know. He didn't want to look at her, touch her, lift her, whatever...*you handle this bitch, Seth...I want no part. It's your trash...you clean up your own fucking mess.*

The echo of his own harsh words pummeled his ears like repeated gunfire at close range. His brain hurt. He couldn't *believe* what he'd just said. He'd never used these words his entire life until now, but somehow the epithets just tumbled uncontrollably from his mouth as if possessed. His fury at Seth was doing it to him. That must be why. He *was* possessed. With rage and disbelief. He felt a stabbing pity for the poor young girl who deserved none of this; remorse too for whatever his brother had probably done. And for his own words. He was sorry and ashamed for his words—they were coming out all wrong! His ire was directed at Seth, not her. He meant those harsh words for him! *I don't know why the fuck I'm saying this shit. It's just kind of pouring out of me.* He felt himself coming unhinged. He tried to calm himself and slow down. OK. OK. No time to panic, Nate. You didn't do anything. This is all your idiot brother's doing. He's got you rattled, thinking unclearly. Just stay focused. Stay calm. Deep breaths. *OK. So.* Nate made a decision: he wasn't going to help Seth load this poor young girl into the Pathfinder. Nor would he help carry her into the emergency room or help try to explain what happened. That was all Seth's responsibility, and Nate wanted *zero* part of it. His decision was that he would drive them to the hospital and drop them off there. That was it. Then they could take a taxi home, or Seth could take one home on his own, or whatever the hell else he wanted to do from that point on. But like he said, in no uncertain terms, *just leave me the fuck out of it.*

Little did Nate or his brother know that right before their panicky exchange, Teresa had started to regain consciousness. That she was emerging from her enveloping black hole, her senses close to the surface. And that she could hear, very clearly, every word the boys said.

A short time before, as she wriggled free of her comatose state, Seth was making a call in another room and hadn't seen her sit up and look around, dumbfounded. It took a few moments to put the pieces of the puzzle together. *The whiskey in the truck. Then something felt wrong. And now she was here. The sports posters she recognized on the wall. It was Seth's room.* She *knew* she'd been violated. She could *sense* it. Hearing Seth's hysterical pleas on the phone just seemed to confirm it for her.

It was now time for Teresa to become the actress she always dreamed she'd be.

She heard the phone call. She heard Seth pacing in the kitchen. She heard his brother's footsteps into the house. And then the dialogue just outside the bedroom where she now lay. She had to remain focused. *Stay limp. Stay sleepy.* She had to hear every word of what they were saying, but stay in a deep, relaxed state. *This is crucial, Teresa. Slow, steady breaths. They don't know you're awake. They think you can't hear them. The rapist and his frozen-hearted brother. Let this asshole pick you up, there you go, stay as limp as possible. Let him put you in the backseat. Relax. Focus, Teresa. Stay calm. This is just a Hollywood thriller. And right now, you're the star. Focus. Calm.*

Outside the emergency room doors, Nate peeled away in the truck, leaving Seth to haul in a still-limp Teresa through the corridor. Once inside, he sat her on the first empty chair he could find, and breathless and panicky, spun around, peppering people with questions. Then he ran up to the admittance window and tried to calmly convey that he thought there might be something wrong with his girlfriend, and he didn't know what to do.

An administrative staff member walked out and asked Seth a series of questions, and his summary of events went something like this:

She's my girlfriend, we were at a party and decided to break away for a drink, then decided to head over to my house to make out, and she wanted us to try some special K with the whiskey, even though I told her I thought it was a bad idea because of combined effects or whatever, but she insisted, so we both took some and then had sex—we had consensual sex—and then she passed out about an hour ago, and now we're here.

Skeptical, the hospital staff placed her in a wheelchair and rolled her into the back, with Seth being told to remain in the waiting area. The doctors were doing whatever they were doing behind closed doors, and Seth had to sweat it out in the waiting room, until finally a staff member ultimately came out and explained that she was awake and responsive, and that she would be released to her parents in a few hours. He could go home.

Fortunately for Seth, Teresa had decided against a rape kit. She feared the results would only end up inconclusive, especially after she had reassembled the puzzle pieces to the day's events. There were drugs and alcohol in her system (she was just told); she ended up at her boyfriend's house (where she'd been several times before); someone probably saw them leave the party together in a rush of excitement. To her, there would just be no way to prove that the very recent sexual relations—which Seth would surely insist were consensual—were, in fact, quite the opposite.

But Teresa knew. She would always know. It would be her special secret. One she would carry with her.

Back at school, the rumor mill was at full strength. That Teresa Reynolds was a hidden drug addict who did serious stuff like ketamine and maybe other stuff, and that was probably why she was always so calm and relaxed and focused-seeming in class. And why she was such a good student and could digest Shakespeare and Greek tragedies like they were Dr. Seuss. That maybe anyone would be, if they had the right drugs to help them lock in to their studies and help them cope with the stresses of high school.

Then there were suggestions about her sexual proclivities, for which nobody had the smallest shred of proof, other than the purported version: that she and Seth had skipped out of the party and dashed over to his house that night to get high and have sex at her request. All it took was one gossipy student who was envious of Teresa. Or had an ax to grind. Regardless, with that version of events swirling around, the hundreds of teenage brains at Stony Ridge High School only found ways to make things worse, embellishing the already fictitious story with additional outrageous details. The rumor mill continued to spin on, creating an increasingly toxic environment for an already distraught, confused, and traumatized Teresa.

The devastating incident had left her psychologically and emotionally scarred. The rape itself was a near-complete blank to her. She could only dredge up bits and pieces from the party, the first drink in the backseat of the truck, and then the aftermath at the house. The hospital ER staff had explained to her that she had a significant amount of ketamine in her system, and that there was possible circumstantial evidence of sexual assault. She had never done any drugs—the thought never even appealed to her—not even a cigarette. As far as sex, she had only had relations that one time the year before with Lucas Portman, and she was *certain* that no matter how much she drank, she would not have willingly had sex with

Seth Daniels. Not at that early stage in their relationship. To her, it was then crystal clear: she was drugged and kidnapped and raped by someone she had trusted, and even at one point she thought had liked quite a bit.

The realization prompted a welter of emotions—shame, guilt, rage, disbelief—and when she went back to school the following week, she fought to reconcile what had happened with what was being whispered about her. In person, previous friends offered her hollow gestures of support and compassion. Away from her presence, though, they now looked upon her with suspicion and low regard. *With friends like that*, she thought...

Teresa couldn't believe all this was happening to her, and one day she broke down in tears at home after school. Her mother (they were divorced and her dad lived elsewhere) was equal parts distraught and furious, but agreed, based on what Teresa had told her, that an attempt to prosecute this vile Seth kid would probably go nowhere. She insisted they should do it anyway, only then to cede to Teresa's stronger insistence that they shouldn't. She just wanted to move on, Teresa said.

"Well, what about counseling or therapy, sweetheart? Would you at least try that?"

"And what's that gonna solve, Ma? Will that change what happened to me or the shit storm that's going on at school? Will it?"

After a few days, and similar exchanges with her school counselor, it was agreed that Teresa should transfer schools to nearby Oak Park High School as soon as possible. It took her time to acclimate, and though Teresa wasn't particularly social during the first few weeks at her new school, she still made an effort to hang out with Jacky on occasion, who, she could sense, was already slowly moving on. Teresa felt like many of their conversations those days were like really bad script lines, lines for a role she would never voluntarily accept. Not as any respectable actress.

"How come we never really get together anymore?" asked Teresa, the last time they spoke. She could feel Jacky avoiding her. "It's been like forever."

"I'm just busy, that's all, OK?" said Jacky. "Listen, I gotta run. Talk to you soon."

"Busy? Now all of a sudden, you're so busy with everything?"

"I'll see ya around, Teresa. Just…just take care of yourself."

A really bad movie, she thought. Well, even bad movies had to end at some time.

Slowly, as months passed, Teresa started to heal and break out of her shell of introversion and guardedness. She became noticeably more animated as the energy-depleting shame, guilt, and despair morphed into some form of hatred and rage that seemed to fuel her. Determined, Teresa was learning to take those very emotions born from her living nightmare and channel their dark energy into more constructive pursuits. She read and studied passionately, first the classics, including Shakespeare and Donne and Milton and Poe, and then whatever else she could get her hands on. She even decided she'd indulge herself and attend an improv class. It was no surprise to her that she excelled, her teacher drawing attention to her talents, telling her she could enjoy a great future as a thespian. More months crawled by, and Teresa graduated. Despite her obvious love and passion for reading and analyzing literary texts, the prospect of college never really held that much appeal for her, and so after high school, she said that what she wanted to do was find work, live at home for a while, and save up money. Then, eventually, she could get her own place. Live on her own.

One day, a friend of her mom's had mentioned to her mother something about becoming a casino dealer of some sort, poker maybe, where a girl like her could make good money. All that was required was a brief stint at training school, and then, as soon as she turned eighteen, she could start gaining experience immediately.

To Teresa, the prospect of working in the casino environment was a welcome one. It even made perfect sense, in a weird way. It wasn't her dream, the way acting was, but that would be put on hold for now. The casino was a strange, dark place where she could better study people. Their movements. Their behaviors. People who would be laughing one second, then barking at another player the next. People who moved about like zombies with pockets full of cash, sometimes gambling away rent or entire savings accounts, often without their spouses having the slightest clue. People were different there. Plus there were secrets revealed at the tables. Dark aspects of people's personalities would creep through the masks they wore when they came in. So to her, it was twofold: she got a closeup, intimate view of the human condition, often at its worst, and with her already gifted hand-eye coordination, natural dexterity, and quick analytical mind, she could quickly perfect her craft, letting her nights just drone on without any emotional energy expended. Meanwhile she could build up a little nest egg. Not a bad scenario, all things considered, she thought.

At her first job, at Pechanga Casino, they allowed the dealers to roll up their long-sleeved uniforms, be it because of excessive heat (though the air-conditioning was usually on), or for added comfort while dealing. As long as they performed their jobs proficiently and with positive attitudes, management didn't care too much. The first few weeks on the job, Teresa had worn her sleeves down and buttoned like pretty much everyone else. The shirt was comfortable enough anyway, especially with the steady stream of cool air from the AC vents.

Then she decided to get the panda tattoo. Just below the wrist of her left hand, the one that held the deck while she dealt. A few days after she got the tattoo, the inflammation had mostly subsided and the edges looked crisp and clear. She occasionally began to roll up her sleeves, so that the panda's black ears and part of its furry head poked out, just enough for Teresa to sneak an occasional glance, an empowering glance, at the symbol that represented for her so many, many things: violation, loss of innocence and trust, but also strength, beauty, softness of spirit, among others. She had thought about getting creative, maybe adding a yin yang with a panda bite taken from the black yang side, or maybe have the panda holding a

Chinese star in one of its paws. As if ready to throw at someone's neck. But ultimately she decided against it, as it would draw too much attention and prompt too many unwanted questions that she had no desire to address. The tattoo was for her, after all. Public inquiries were just an unfortunate by-product of its beautiful artistry and the cuddly association most people had with gentle, loving pandas. Who didn't, really? Pandas were adorable little creatures that harmed no one and just snacked away on their little bamboo shoots. To Teresa, it was now also a permanent symbol of disgust and hatred and rage, and ultimately, she knew, a revenge she would one day exact. This panda, with its two black eyes, would help her heal, and then look in Teresa's own pained eyes, urging her to do what was necessary to make her feel whole again.

TURN

TURN

Steal:
A raise by someone in late position in an attempt to reduce the number of players and/or to steal the pot

STEAL

When Trigger snapped on the second of two rubber gloves once inside the apartment, he knew he had a window of about forty-five minutes to be in and out, money and all, his tracks neatly covered. Of course, the first step involved actually *locating* the vault. Unlocking it would be no gimme, either. And while Ivan and Monica were both confirmed to be out, they apparently had gone separately and to different locations. That could always pose a potential problem. Yet to Trigger, it was highly unlikely that either would return within the hour, based on who they were with and where they had gone. He had done his homework.

He challenged himself: he thought he'd need no more than twenty minutes to both find and unlock the vault, take the stash and then cover all his tracks. So that was the mark he would shoot for.

So far so good.

He had timed the front-desk switch perfectly, as planned. The outgoing employee at 4:58 p.m. bolted like he had a plane to catch, and the incoming guy was too concerned about settling down and unwrapping the aluminum foil from his early dinner. No one in the lobby seemed to pay much attention to Trigger in his dirty hat and plumber's jumpsuit with a *Joe* pouch stitched on the front breast pocket. Then he made sure to take the back stairs, eliminating a possible elevator encounter with a resident.

And now, he was in Ivan's apartment, gloves on, the door relocked behind him. The duplicate key worked without a hitch—he still couldn't believe how easy it was for Teresa to make a clay impression of Ivan's front door key so they could make a copy. *So this is how the prick lives these days*, he thought, scanning the apartment. *Ivan Fucking Parker. Some piece of work, you are.* He snapped back to the task at hand. *OK, pricko, well let's hope opening your safe goes just as smoothly.*

But first things first. Which was actually *finding* the safe.

Where exactly was it? They were pretty certain it had to be in the vicinity of the southeast wall, opposite the dining room table, as it was from that wall where Teresa said she had noticed Ivan almost break his neck and babble like a child. She told Trigger the story—something along the lines of: "Nice painting, Ivan. New?" Teresa had asked. "Oh…uh…no…I mean, yeah…uh, just picked it up," all stammering and nervous, forcing himself to not even look in that direction.

So it was likely to be behind the painting, Teresa told him, or at least in that vicinity.

And so it was.

He paused to remember his first fascination with computers and basic programming. He had a knack. That was obvious to him after even his first class at the institute. But little did he know that one day he would become an expert at finding the back doors and unguarded portals to other people's computers.

To their assumed, safeguarded personal information. E-mails, browser histories, passwords, just about anything really. All that was needed was the right skill set and a little creativity, and you could get your hands on almost anything. Even after Ivan had screwed him over, he never imagined it would be his computer savvy that might one day be Ivan's undoing. He just thought it was a fun trick to be able to hack in and steal other people's stuff...

Back to work.

He used a dining-room chair to prop himself up and then carefully slid the weighty piece off the thick nails in the wall and placed it gently against the floor to the side. He saw a crevice in the wall. *That could only be Ivan's little vault,* he thought. He ran his gloved finger along the crevice and then lightly pressed against the wall, looking for a little spring latch—*click.* A thin panel popped open and swung out neatly from the wall, exposing the brushed steel face of a digital safe and a thin vertical handle that jutted out from the safe's face. *Nice piece of machinery, pal.* He pressed the six-digit combination he had lifted from Ivan's computer days before, *hacker extraordinaire that he was,* and pulled the handle to open the safe. Nothing happened. Panic crept in, as Trigger closed his eyes and forced himself to project, in big pink neon numbers onto the black screen of his closed eyes, the combination he was sure he had memorized correctly. There was literally no way he could've forgotten them. *Any chance Ivan changed the combo for some reason, but then forgot to store it in the keychain on his computer? God, I fucking hope not.* He saw the neon numbers crackling big and bright against the black backdrop: 7 2 9 3 0 2. He tried them again. Slowly: 7

2 9 3 0 2. This time he made sure to press each number in the center of the button and at a nice easy pace and—*presto!*—the vault beeped and popped open. He curled his fingers around the metal handle and pulled open the safe door wide, immediately struck by the strong scent of bundled cash that washed over him and seeped through his nostrils. *Pay dirt,* he thought. *And payback too, scumbag. Though this is just the beginning. Better hang on tight.* He was really starting to have some fun.

He took the thin nylon bag, crumpled up in his oversize pants pocket, and started emptying all the bricks of cash into the bag. The sudden increase in weight and heft of the contents felt by his left arm prompted a smile. He looked at his watch. Another smile. He still had time to go to the fridge and make a damn peanut butter and jelly sandwich if he wanted, and *still* have time to burn. Instead, he nudged the safe door closed and shut the latch, ensuring it was flush with the wall. Then he gently guided the cash-swollen bag down to the floor and grabbed the painting with two hands by the top edge, setting the thick steel wire across its back softly onto the exposed nailheads in the wall.

After replacing the dining-room chair, he checked for any sign or hint of his having been there. *Nothing,* he said to himself, *oh well nothing, other than the now empty safe and, as a parting gift, the evil hex I'm now placing on your apartment and life.* Satisfied, he made his way out the door, locking it behind him, and then slithered down the hall, crept down the stairs to the lobby, and slid out the side door, without being seen by another soul.

Ivan came home about thirty-five minutes later, his wife two hours after that. No one was the wiser.

Busted:
An incomplete draw that never fills, in the case of a straight or flush; also a reference to when a poker player loses all his or her chips

BUSTED

Sam couldn't believe his own eyes. It was actually him! That bartender from years ago in Chicago at the Buddha Lounge… no. Sound-bar. Yes. That real suave dude in the middle of the hot-chick hurricane, he vaguely remembered calling it. What was his name? What was it? It had some Spanish or Italian ring to it, like Rocco or Mateo. It was definitely him though. Same spiky hair—maybe a bit longer now—and scruffy face. Marco! That was it! He recalled the very moment years ago in the club when Christina had broken his trance and told him and Griff that the bartender's name was Marco. He still had that cocky air about him. And he was just a couple of tables over.

Sam folded the hand he was dealt and got up to walk over to the poker desk, requesting a table change to table seven. Any other tables if they open up? Nope just seven please. Thanks. OK, we'll let you know.

He went back to his seat and got lost in the reverie of the years that had passed since his first Marco sighting at Sound-bar. It was his birthday, he remembered. The big 2–0. About three and a half years ago to date. Since then he'd gotten a job waiting tables at Roscoe's, scraped together a starter bankroll and spent a few enjoyable evenings with Griff at a nearby casino to sharpen his poker game. Whenever Griff got tied up, Sam just coolly made the trip on his own. Every spare dollar Sam got his greedy hands on was either poured into poker books or wrapped tightly around his playing roll. And as his game continued to improve, often little by little, occasionally by quantum leaps, his bankroll likewise began to swell.

The way he appeared for work each day in the cafe, haggard and drowsy from little sleep, the Mexican employees sensed he had been up all night playing poker. So it became somewhat of a shift-starting ritual, as they eagerly prodded him for details of his nocturnal expeditions.

"Hey, gringo, how much you win last night?" was a typical greeting from Jorge, a busser who worked alongside Sam during those days.

"Been on a roll lately, amigo," was a typical reply from Sam.

He regaled the guys almost daily with a few colorful details, believing that was all they were really after. Yet Sam discovered these small sample offerings just prompted them to ask more and more, unsated as they were for a window into that mysterious world where such easy money could be made.

Eventually, since Sam was just *crushing it* at the tables, he came to see the job as superfluous and nonsensical, often making more in a night than in a week at the cafe. And so he quit and began playing poker full-time. It felt inevitable. He knew it was a risky move, but so was working in some bullshit job for the next five to ten years, having to tolerate the tedium and drudgery, his emotional well-being under fire with each passing day.

Luckily, he was able to make do. And then some. He won on a consistent basis, feeling increasingly confident to keep raising the stakes. And when he kept playing bigger and winning bigger, he decided to move into his own place in Lincoln Park. He'd always liked the vibe there and recalled thinking it was the perfect spot for him. Well, at least in the summer it was perfect, along with a few other thin slices of the year, when he tended to spend his days riding his bike down by the lakeshore or strolling around the neighborhood, having tea or coffee with a friend, maybe taking his sketchbook and drawing for a couple of hours until it was time to go drive out to the riverboats in Indiana and play poker. Occasionally, he'd be invited to a home game or two, which was, after all, where he got his start.

But that last winter, Chicago's appeal shivered right out of his frozen bones. Those cold, sharp, wintry bolts of air kept puncturing any and all belief that Sam could spend *even one more cold ass* season there. So he did his research, looking into the poker scene and apartment prices on both coasts. The ultimate conclusion: it would be sunshine and poker or bust. Florida had a nice warm ring to it. The way he heard it, poker was just picking up steam in South Florida, as the state had just passed some broadening laws, and those with plenty of wealth (but few outlets for legalized gambling) were impatient to start tossing it around at the poker tables. He considered California too, but saw that rental prices were pretty steep, while the quality of poker there was rumored at that time to be kind of hit or miss.

And so here was Sam now, over three years later. *Tan as a mofo.* Some days called for the beach, others the pool. Occasionally he'd spend his afternoons biking through the palm-tree-lined streets. Anything and everything to get sun on his face and every other tannable body part, as he noticed the marrow in his bones gratefully begin to thaw. The bitingly cold daggers that swept off Lake Michigan were a thing of the past. And the girls out there in Florida were ridiculous. He didn't even know where to start.

He tried out a few local casinos and eventually decided on a small apartment in Fort Lauderdale. From there, he'd commute to play poker each night at the Hard Rock in Hollywood, about twenty miles north. The drive wasn't too bad, as he got to rock out with his badass sound system in his new BMW, and was always shocked at how quickly the trip just seemed to fly by.

He first started playing four to five days a week, convincing himself he should take nights off to avoid burnout. Then he realized he was winning so much and so often that each night spent at home felt like gobs of money just left on the table. So he started playing seven days a week, making a point to invest just an hour or two at the tables on some days, especially if he found himself getting tired or distracted. Maybe head over with a friend to a bar at the hotel or another nearby bar or club in the area.

<<Hey, Sammy, you still want a table change to seven? OK. Go ahead—seat eight is open.>>

Seat eight. Directly across from seat three. Where one bottle-flipping, spiky-haired Marco sat, a broad pile of pink and orange and purple and black chips in front of him. *Damn, is he really that good at poker too?* Not surprisingly, Sam decided he would dedicate every chance he got to examining this guy and breaking him down as much as possible. If for no other reason, Sam thought, than to boost his own ego by winning a huge pot off him and proving to himself that he (Sam) was a better player. Marco can't have all the looks and all the girls *and* all the skills, Sam thought. *We'll see what you're made of, my friend.*

Almost immediately, Sam could tell that Marco looked nervous. He wasn't even playing that many hands, and when he handled his chips or inspected his little chip pouch, his fingers started to fumble a bit. There was something awkward about him. Sam also noticed that Marco was always taking the third chip from the top of his big chips to put in the pot. Never the top one or second down. He'd grab the top three, act like he was deep in thought and then turn those three upside down, betting the only top one. If you had no reason to suspect anything, it might just seem quirky. The guy had a shitload of chips, after all. But something was up, Sam knew. He would certainly find out one way or another. Nobody else seemed to notice but him. He looked around at the other players at the table, thinking: *Do you guys even know how to win in this game?* Now it was certainly getting fun.

At some point, after about a half hour of relative inactivity, Sam watched as Marco stood up and shuffled over to the bathroom. A few uneventful minutes passed, and Sam snagged a glimpse of Marco rubbing his forehead on his way back, as if something weighed heavily on his mind. Then Marco slid his chip pouch out from his front pocket and plucked out another pink and two orange chips—*another seven thousand!*—his head on a swivel like he was watching a tennis match at midcourt. *Why you so nervous, Marco buddy? Very fishy*, thought Sam. It wasn't like Marco had lost a big pot or anything and had to re-load. Sam decided he needed to take action. He needed to find out what was at the heart of Marco's odd behavior. Sam vowed that he would be proactive and take down the next decent-size pot Marco entered; he'd do whatever was necessary to win it. Even risk a big bluff, if that's what was required. Then he'd have Marco's chips to inspect up close. *I have to know. It'll be worth it.*

Teresa's rotation swung her around to table nine, where she got a clear view of both Nate at table six and Marco at table seven. It didn't take her long to spot Sam viewing Marco with an unusual measure of doubt or suspicion. She made a mental note to check back on the situation to see if anything developed.

Fifteen minutes later, it happened. Sam's chance. Seat one raised preflop. Marco reraised, and it was folded around to Sam, who decided he wouldn't even look at this hand until he had to, maybe not at all. Sam called. Other guy called. Flop came out. Checked over to Marco. He made a continuation bet. Sam called. Other guy folded. Marco bet big on the turn, and Sam decided he was gonna raise big here, just enough to force Marco to hopefully put some orange chips in the middle, but not so much that he wouldn't be able to shove all in on the river and bluff Marco off the hand. Sam still hadn't looked at his cards and didn't even care. Marco thought for a few moments and called and then checked to Sam on the river. Sam followed through with his plan, pushing all in. Marco screwed up his face and muttered something under his breath, folding nearly thirty seconds later. Sam kept his eyes locked on the thousand-dollar orange chips Marco put in the pot. The dealer pushed the pot over to Sam, and he swept the pot toward him, casually lifting an orange chip and placing it to the side, feeling a chill of excitement as he readied himself for a closer examination.

At this point, Teresa had really keyed in on Sam, the guy with the mangled left hand, who was indisputably inspecting an orange chip, his face twisted with suspicion. She knew she had to help pull the plug on the whole operation, before an ugly scene ensued and Nate possibly got snagged too. *That's not how it's supposed to go at all*, she thought, anxious now.

"Seat eight, big blind honey," said Fran, the dealer at table seven, to the young guy in seat eight.

Yeah, he's super distracted, thought Teresa. *He knows.* "Hey, Bobby, can you sit in for me a few hands real quick?"

"You OK?" asked Bobby, passing by her table.

"Yeah, but I *really* need a quick bathroom break—sorry the hot tea kinda caught up with me all a sudden. Thanks, hon."

Teresa skipped over in the direction of the restroom area and then veered off quickly, yanking out her cellphone. She texted Nate: "Hey, pick up ur chips and cash out right now—not in 2 mins...right now! Marco's caught!"

After a few seconds, Sam knew he had him. Both the orange and purple chips he scooped off Marco felt different from his own of the same color. The slightest difference, really. *Was the hue of this one off a bit?* Yeah, maybe. *How about the weight?* He closed his eyes and considered. Yeah, the weight was iffy too. However slight the difference between the chips, and it was certainly minimal, it didn't matter. Sam at that point knew for sure that these very chips stood out. Phony, probably, and likely the same few ones Marco added on his way back from the bathroom. Sam was a master of calculating odds on the spot, and in his estimation, he figured it was about a 90–95 percent likelihood Marco was knowingly using counterfeit chips. *Should I rat on him?* he wondered. Sam had in all likelihood unveiled Marco's ploy, but could he derive an even deeper satisfaction by relaying the juicy news to Paul, the night manager on duty? By knocking Sam's one-time idol off his goddamn pedestal once and for all? Maybe the staff would be incredibly appreciative too. *Pretty ironic*, he thought. *The shy, quiet guy with the missing fingers, fingering the hot-shot, wannabe rock star, or whatever the hell he was.* Of course, Sam then wouldn't be able to cash out the decoy chips. Or maybe the casino staff would redeem them after they verified Sam's innocence. But none of that really mattered right now. All he needed was one more small reason to get up and do it; one tiny impetus to spring him out of his chair...And there it was! Another snide look from Marco over to him—he just couldn't bear the fact that the cripple was eyeballing him the whole time and beating his ass out of big pots. *You shady motherfucker, Marco. What are you involved with, you prick?*

Suddenly an old memory bubbled up from the depths of Sam's consciousness. It was his old pal Griff, yelling in his ear by the bar that night, "Don't worry, Sammie, someday you'll take his punk ass down." At the time, as he recalled it, Sam was baffled by the remark. But no longer. Now it was merely a call to action. *Yes indeed, Griffin, buddy. Yes indeed.*

Ahem. "Oh, Paul…"

On Tilt:
Playing worse (usually more aggressively) than usual because a player has become emotionally upset

ON TILT

My son is something of an angel, thought Naomi Sharpe, virtually every time she looked at her only child. She had even spoken this very description to friends and acquaintances, standing alongside Cathy and Vic Greene, or Fran and Ronnie Hammels, or numerous other Elysian Valley neighborhood guests at birthday parties or visits to Echo Park. Marco is just very kind and loving, she would add. Respectful to his parents and any guests who would swing by the house. Even after Naomi and Glen had divorced, Glen moving a whole world away to the opposite coast in South Florida, young Marco, while crushed, seemed to hold on to this childlike joy and exuberance.

His mom had a few brief relationships after that, but nothing really lasted. Her heart just didn't seem to be in it. Naomi might've still been shaken by the split with her high-school sweetheart with whom she once thought she'd grow old and die. But she still lived for her son, and much of the time, it was just the two of them together, alone in the little white house in Los Angeles. She worked from home, alternating between various graphic design jobs on her computer and quality time with her son. When she wasn't working, the two of them would laugh and carry on about a fateful winning roll in a game of backgammon, or battle it out to the bloody end in Stratego, Marco's favorite board game. Naomi could only smile when her son would cry out to her, "Mom, how many times do I have to beat you until you try a different setup?" He thought his mom might be letting him win sometimes but couldn't tell for sure. It didn't matter, really. They both had too much fun enjoying each other's company to even care who won. Other empty hours found mom and son camped out on the couch, taking in cool TV detective shows like *Law and Order*, and movie thrillers like *Memento* and *Fight Club* that delightfully messed with Marco's head. Some days, they would listen to jazz together, tapping their feet to Coltrane or the Bird, while they consulted the used book that taught them about rhythm and syncopation. *A cool word*, Marco thought. Syncopation: where they played *off the beat*. Long bike rides were common too, as they loved the time spent outdoors in the warm sun, pedaling together down Ripple Street or through Echo Park, both eagerly anticipating that day's first taste of pistachio ice cream on their tongues, at that great neighborhood spot that stocked homemade. Some nights found Marco helping out in the kitchen with some of his mom's special recipes. Especially chicken parm, which was his favorite—as he would tell anyone and everyone who would listen. He even offered to do extra work on chicken parm days, like brushing on the extra virgin olive oil and spicy Italian tomato sauce, then sprinkling on with messy fingers the light bread crumb crust and great gobs of shredded mozzarella cheese. These were special times. He loved nothing more in the world than his mom, and the days and months and years they spent together as Marco grew up were those they both cherished deeply.

One day, Marco thought he heard his mom in a coughing fit, from behind the closed bathroom door.

"Mom, you OK?"

"Yeah, Marco honey, just a little bug, I think. I'll be OK. Just tired and need to relax."

"Are you hurting? You don't look good."

"I'm fine, honey, just a bit tired…maybe I'll take a nap on the couch."

"Do you want me to cook us dinner while you nap?" asked the eleven-year-old Marco.

"Uh…no, sweetie, that's very thoughtful, but I'm not hungry. Why don't you order something to get delivered—whatever you want, pizza, Thai food, fish tacos. The menus are in the middle drawer next to the dishwasher. Just not chicken parm—save that for when we make it together."

His mom wasn't one to ever complain or mention feeling sick. Marco could maybe only recall her suffering from a cold once and maybe a short bout with the flu a few years back. So he felt concerned. He would always when it came to his mom, as she was the world to him. Though if she insisted that she was fine, then he shouldn't worry. She must be fine. Marco was relieved: he knew he could trust whatever she told him.

The next day, however, she seemed to be anything but fine, her coughing almost nonstop. She hurried him to get in the car because they had to go to see a doctor. A doctor? But all she had was a little cough. Still, they jumped in the 2006 Maserati—the one Naomi got in the divorce settlement—and drove ten minutes east on Riverside Drive to the doctor. While his mom went into a closed exam room to speak to the doctor, Marco sat in the waiting room with his book about a bank heist gone bad. There was a murder. A brilliant detective too. Really nasty-type characters. He got so lost in his story that he forgot why he was even sitting in the area outside a doctor's office. If asked, he wouldn't have been able to say whether it had been five minutes or forty-five minutes that had passed. This book was *that* good. He looked up and saw his mom walking back out into the waiting room, a white-jacketed middle-aged doctor a few steps behind her. Like the characters in his novel would often do, Marco tried to read his mom's expression for clues. Then the doctor's. As far as his keen detective eye could tell, neither seemed to be overly concerned. So neither was he.

His mom explained to him in the car that this doctor couldn't find anything wrong with her. But that she and Marco would have to take another trip to see a different doctor. A *specialist*, she said.

"But, Mom, if this this doctor you just went to said he saw nothing wrong, why would another doctor know any better?" asked Marco.

"Because, honey," said his mom between coughs, "this other doctor has some high-tech machines that can maybe see what this doctor couldn't see."

"Is it dangerous? Could it hurt?" Marco asked, concerned.

"No, I think it's perfectly safe," she said, just before being seized by another violent coughing fit. She felt as if punched by invisible blows in the stomach, her hand over her mouth and face turned toward the driver's side window, straining to still watch the road. "We just have to find out why Mom's cough is so bad."

The results of the initial CT scan weren't promising. Another day, another waiting room for Marco, whiling away the minutes with his brilliant detective who was putting together the puzzle pieces of the crime. Today, though, he felt distracted somehow, unable to focus on the pages, his attention pulled in various directions, as if attached by strings of varying lengths and tensions to both the front-desk clerk and her phone, which would ring at odd, constant intervals, and to all the swinging doors and their staccato clicks as they opened and closed, muffled conversations between doctors and patients leaking out. He felt uneasy for some strange reason he couldn't identify and had to rub his eyes really hard with the palms of his hands in an attempt to shake it all away. There was a kaleidoscope of circling stars, similar to the one he used to look through in amazement as a little boy, only it was now colorless and ugly. That, paired with a queasy pit in his stomach. The feeling was unusual for him—it felt oddly similar to the sensation he had just before his mom sat him down to inform him of his parents' divorce. Dread? Was that the right word for it?

His mom appeared from the hallway and then shuffled into the waiting room, her face angled down as if she were studying the carpet, her arms crossed as if cold. This time, Marco's read was different. His mom's eyes seemed red and puffy, her makeup a bit runny, like she'd been crying. The doctor's face betrayed something as well, though he couldn't exactly identify the emotion. Marco froze in swelling panic and his book toppled to the floor, his current chapter's pages bent back sharply, the paper dust jacket slipping off the hard cardboard edges. He didn't even notice.

"Mom? Everything OK? Why are you so upset?"

"Yeah, honey," said his mom. "We'll talk about it in the car."

But, as his mother knew, and as Marco sensed, everything was *not* OK. There would have to be another test to further confirm the specialist's early diagnosis, but the outlook at this point was grim. Stage 3 lung cancer.

Naomi didn't care about the pain or discomfort—she could tolerate all that—along with whatever treatment they saw fit to subject her to. She had found a way to finally quit smoking Marlboro Reds when Marco was conceived, but before that she was enslaved to a two- to three-pack-a-day habit for so many years she'd lost count. She deeply regretted it, but right now her main concern was Marco and his long-term welfare. What if the worst of the worst actually happened to her, and she was no longer there for him? His father loved him, sure, but he had amply proved to Naomi over the years that his parenting skills were so lacking that his raising Marco would be unthinkable. She had to somehow make it through this for her son.

For Marco, each new trip to another doctor meant a new welter of thoughts and emotions. He became increasingly worried and morose, his spirit sinking a little every day. He thought he should go ride his bike, but then felt wrong about it, guilty somehow, while his mother was sick and was confined to the couch or her bed. Even eating—he decided he'd give up chicken parm until his mom had the appetite to eat it with him. She only wanted bananas, rice, and potatoes, explaining to him that everything else tasted metallic. Like pocket change, she'd said. Marco couldn't imagine eating food that tasted like that, so for now he would eat bananas, rice, and potatoes too.

Naomi's insurance had covered most of the immediate treatment of chemotherapy and radiation. She consented to whatever they suggested, so desperate was she to rub out this living-nightmare scenario. She started with the first cycle of chemo, driving to the hospital late morning or early afternoon when Marco was at school, then heading home to sip on chicken broth or nibble on a banana or some rice as she waited for Marco to get home. The treatment was outlandishly expensive, she thought, but with her generous divorce settlement money and what she'd been able to sock away for years from her once-thriving graphic-design business, she was confident that it would last the two of them while she took time off from work. But as the time went on and weeks of intensive treatment turned into months, the mounting costs that insurance didn't cover were slowly depleting their once-safe nest egg.

One day, Marco walked into the living room after school and saw his mom crying on the couch.

"Mom, what is it?"

"It's just money I'm concerned about, sweetie. Everything is so expensive, and I wanna make sure we're gonna have enough money." Naomi forced a smile. It wasn't just about money. But she felt she had to spare Marco from the real emotional pain for as long as she could. "Maybe I'm just a little tired and cranky, that's all, Marco. It'll be OK."

That was all Marco needed to hear. He decided he would help out by getting a job after school, working for the Sullivans down the street. Each day he would get off the bus and walk or even run the two short blocks to the small green house on the corner. Nancy and Ted had always been friendly people and particularly nice to Marco whenever they all got together, but it seemed now their beneficence had suddenly ticked up a few notches. They agreed to pay Marco fifty dollars every day—*fifty bucks!*—to spend those few midafternoon hours cleaning the perpetually messy garage or dusty, file-strewn attic or watering the flowers and pulling up weeds in the garden, picking up leaves, cutting the grass. Even painting the side of the house, an area that Marco noted didn't really need much painting. Fifty bucks a day! Marco was sure that this would help his mom get better.

He didn't mind the work, particularly because he thought he was contributing to his mom's treatment and ultimate cure. He even came home one day, knees stained with dirt and pea-green paint smudges on his beige T-shirt, crisp bills in his front pocket. He talked breathlessly about how he was going to quit school and get another job, maybe work in the bakery down the street that made those mouth-watering chocolate croissants, or maybe bus tables at the coffee shop that served his mom's favorite cappuccinos.

His mom obviously wouldn't hear of it, dismissing his ideas as gently as she could. There was no real way for Marco to know that it was precisely his future that Naomi cared about the most.

"Out of the question, my sweet little Energizer bunny," said his mom. "It's nice enough you're doing what you're doing with the Sullivans."

He needed to follow through with his education, maybe go to college, even become a professional of some sort. Plus she knew what Marco couldn't—that his contribution, while heartfelt, was really just a symbolic gesture in the face of the gargantuan medical bills that were tallying up.

The fact that they struggled to hold on to what little they had was compounded by Marco's dad and his constant grumbling that his business was really hurting, that he was struggling to pay even his own mortgage, plus what he already had to give Naomi. That *he* was really dealing with major money issues too, not just them. All this Marco gleaned from the angry phone calls his mom occasionally had those days with his dad.

After about three months, the expensive treatment wasn't working as they had hoped, so Naomi decided to give it a break and look for a plausible alternative treatment. Herbs, acupuncture, reiki—she tried everything she could think of, had read about, or was suggested to her by supportive neighborhood friends. All to little effect. Until one day a man called her cellphone, introducing himself as Dr. Perkins. He explained that a mutual friend of theirs had given him their number. That he was optimistic he could help.

"Oh," Naomi said, surprised, though encouraged. "Who was that?"

"Jim Lambert," the man responded. "Good man."

"Oh, OK, nice of him, I guess." She paused for a brief coughing fit. "What's this about?"

"Well, Mrs. Sharpe, l am board certified in internal medicine, specializing mostly in holistic cancer treatments, and I've developed a revolutionary treatment that might interest you… it's somewhat of a secret because it hasn't yet been approved yet by AMA/FDA, but they tend to be overly cautious. I assure you we've had great success with shrinking tumors in a number of patients who hadn't found relief with traditional allopathic methods."

After the phone call, Naomi folded the torn sheet of paper on which she'd scribbled the doctor's name and address, and then briefly described to her son what this new specialist had told her. Marco, himself weary from his mom's declining health and battles with chemotherapy and radiation, only retained parts of what she told him. He just remembered that this doctor had some kind of breakthrough or revolutionary treatment, and since the other treatments weren't working particularly, and were making his mom sick and destroying her quality of life on top of it, this had to be worth a shot.

To Naomi too, it was worth a shot. It was expensive, but what wasn't when it came to battling cancer. At first, there were signs of encouragement, as she seemed to feel better, especially when this apparent miracle worker had shown her fresh printout results of several tests he ran, showing what he called *definitive proof* that her tumors were shrinking.

"Are you sure these are accurate?" Naomi asked the doctor on several occasions, optimistic, but skeptical. "I mean, I think I did feel better that first week or so, but now I'm not so sure I feel much different."

"Mrs. Sharpe, trust me. This is my specialty. These print-outs are showing the signs of tumor shrinkage we were hoping for."

But weeks rolled into months, and after that initial glow of optimism, her symptoms kept getting more severe, despite the doctor's repeated assurances that it might get a bit worse before it got better. *But coughing up blood and sputum*, she thought, her optimism morphing into incredulity and despair. *Wasn't that a major concern?*

And then, as suddenly as the so-called doctor had popped into her life, he disappeared, along with his office, his number, and his other patients. Gone. Vanished. Not a note.

A call to Jim Lambert had them both scratching their heads. Not only didn't he have any way to reach any Dr. Perkins, he had no earthly idea who or what she was talking about.

"I'm really so extremely sorry, Naomi, but I never referred any doctor or specialist to you. The guy was obviously lying."

"Are you sure? Even a casual mention to someone who might've then gotten my number?"

"I'm sure. Again, I'm sorry you had to go through that, Naomi."

Jim ended the call by offering to lend her any assistance; anything he could do for her or her son—that for her to just let him know, anytime. She could almost feel his raw, poorly disguised pity seep out from the little holes on the phone, the same way she could hear her heart crack down the middle, like the crunching of thin glass under someone's shoe.

One blustery winter day, away from all the doctors and hospitals, Marco on the brown fuzzy couch opposite his mom, Naomi told her son they needed to have an important chat. Unseasonably cold winter air snuck through the cracks in the windowpanes. Marco felt a chill and pit in his stomach, like the time...

"About what, Mom?"

"Marco, my dear son, the absolute love of my life. You know you've always been an angel to me."

She'd been crying again, he noticed. *Uh oh.*

"I'm sure you've heard me brag about you to the neighbors a million times, right?"

"I guess so, yeah," said Marco, at a loss as to where his mom was going with this, though hoping desperately it was just some small thing about school or clothes or whatever. But somehow knowing that it wasn't.

"Well, now that my health is failing and...um...well, we have to face it—Mom might not live too much longer," Naomi began.

Marco shuddered, imagining another cold, angry, wintry gust growling at the window as it slipped through a crack in the pane and squeezed him in its frosty embrace. He noticed it was hard to focus.

"We have to face the truth here, my love," said Naomi. "No matter how much it hurts. I'm going to die. And life will be much different for you." She let him cry for a few seconds and then handed him some tissues. "And it's OK to cry and grieve. All that will help you heal. But..." Now she was losing her own struggle against her emotions, and against the violent cough that echoed through the living room. Tears continued to stream down Marco's now crumpled-up face. Naomi hugged her son close and grabbed a nearby box of tissues with her free hand from the wooden coffee table. "It's OK, Marco. Let it out. Let it out. That's it."

Marco looked at his mom through a fog of tears, but couldn't think of anything to say. The cold, swirling wind blew hard at the front door. A loose board rattled. Metal chimes tinkled in the distance. He felt like it was a storm, but couldn't tell if it was outside or inside.

"But also, my love, you're going to experience a wide range of emotions you're not accustomed to, because you're so young, and because of your inherent...your inner goodness and light. Don't lose that quality, honey. Protect it, guard it with all your might. Promise me, Marco."

His mom was offering some sort of sound advice, he knew. But it was like watching one of those grown-up TV shows that didn't land right on his ears. Unintelligible words and phrases and ideas. It just wasn't getting through to him. From her own perspective, she just had to get this all out while she could, some sort of emotional purging, before she lost the heart to do so. She knew her son wouldn't grasp everything she was saying. But maybe one word, one phrase, one concept would stay with him. Help him navigate through the inevitable pain and suffering.

"Promise me you won't let those negative emotions—like pain or anger or hatred—never let them consume you, change your inner spirit and goodness. Promise me, OK? Maybe I won't be here with you physically, in person, but in spirit I will always be. You are and always will be my pride and joy. I will look down on you from heaven and help guide you to make the right decisions. I'll always be there. Just promise me you won't give in to the darkness."

He heard the last part clearly, as if his mom had shouted it directly in his ear. *Give in to the darkness?* "Mom, what do you mean?" asked Marco heaving and sniffling. "Why would I ever turn bad? What do you mean darkness? I don't understand. Why would I change?"

"Well, my love," said Naomi, now coughing into a handful of tissues, "tell me how you feel about Mom getting sick. Do you think it's fair?" She thought if she broke it down in this way, it might help clarify some of the issues for him.

Marco hesitated to answer, trying to calm himself down and really focus on what his mom meant. He winced when the loose board rattled again.

Naomi added, "What about the hospitals and the treatments that made Mom suffer, but didn't really help at all? And the fake doctor who just stole our money? How does all that make you feel? Sad, right? But maybe also very, very angry? Like you lost trust and faith in people and the world? And maybe hate everyone?"

"Yeah, I guess. All of those." Those things really did make him angry.

"Well that's what I mean, sweetheart. Those are emotions that, if they stay with you, can really change a person. And I hate to talk about all this, but I just wanna prepare you for what's going to happen soon. When your mom passes away, how it's going to make you feel."

Even if it killed her right then and there, Naomi was determined to get this out. For her son's benefit or her own. She wasn't sure anymore.

"These emotions, if you don't get them all out can change an angel like you into something else. That's what I could never accept. You must know that everybody in the world suffers at some point, that everyone is tested by things that make them really sad or angry or bitter. The world is a big and often crazy place, and sometimes bad things happen to good people. But also know that there are millions and millions of people across the world who get cured of all different types of conditions and diseases because of really smart, caring doctors and nurses in hospitals and clinics. It's not their fault they couldn't cure me. They tried their best. Your mom's disease was...was just too strong. Do you understand this, Marco? Do you understand, sweetie?"

"Um, yeah, I think so." He grabbed another fistful of tissues for the snot that kept running down his nose.

"And Marco, even the fake doctor. There are mean, bad people in the world too ready to take advantage of people, especially when they're most vulnerable. But that doesn't mean most people out there aren't kind and generous and helpful. Like the Sullivans or the Greenes on this street. Aren't they very kindhearted people who go out of their way to help?"

Marco nodded. His mom was making sense. Not everyone was bad. He knew that. Naomi reached for another few tissues while inspecting her son's face for a show of comprehension. She sensed that maybe it was all starting to seep in.

"I know this is a lot for you to take in right now, and much of it you might forget. There's a saying that time heals all wounds. And it's true. As time passes you'll eventually start to feel better. Remember that your mom in heaven once told you that. And to remain the angel that you are now." She held Marco's head close to hers and looked deep into his teary, bloodshot eyes. "Promise me, OK."

"K, Mom, I promise."

"Here, lemme wipe your messy face and that snotty nose, dripping everywhere."

"Mom?"

"Yeah, Marco?"

"Do you ever wish you never met Dad?" Marco surprised himself with the thought.

"Oh, honey. How can I, my love? He's not like you—he doesn't have your inner light or glow, but because I met him and married him, we created you. And you're the best thing to ever happen to me. The eleven years I got to spend with you were better than a thousand I might've spent with someone I didn't care about as much. You must know this, Marco. Your mom loves you so very much, with every ounce of her being and will continue to, long after this disease wins this battle. The word regret—do you know what that means?"

"Like you wish you didn't do something?"

"Exactly. My only regret is not getting to spend another fifty years with you alive. Smoking obviously is a big regret—but I was young, and really stupid. I should have known, but didn't. It was my one big mistake. Really the only one. But there's nothing I can do about it now, so I try to let go of the regret, the wish that I never did it."

"I think I understand, Mom," Marco said.

"I love you to death, kiddo. Give Mom another big hug."

"Love you too, Mom. More than anything. Even when you're in heaven too."

Three weeks later, Marco would attend his mom's funeral, escorted and consoled on both sides by his aunt Helena and uncle Tom. Naomi's fighting spirit had ceded to the inevitable, while Marco's gave way to a crushing grief. Despite hearing his mom's words echo in his mind, he was overcome by this sadness, crippled by it, losing interest in all things, save for long stretches staring at the changing images on his aunt Helena's television screen. His aunt had lost her older sister, and so she too was devastated. But she was sharply aware of the earth-shattering effect it must be having on an eleven-year-old boy, whose mom occupied such an enormous role in his young life. Helena and Tom decided to have Marco stay with them in their house in Pasadena until some other arrangement could be figured out.

Eventually, as the days and months rolled by, the despair blotting out Marco's once-shining spirit started to lift, allowing his pained heart to finally start to mend. He could actually go out and play. Ride his bike or go play ball at the park with friends. Even share cooking duties with his aunt, his desire to have chicken parm gradually rekindled.

But something had changed. Shifted inside him. He couldn't define it at first, but it became more apparent to him with the passing years. He developed a sort of protective shell—a cool, detached demeanor, the expansive and joyful childlike qualities seemingly buried along with his beloved mom. Marco would later think of it as some giant cloud formation in the deep blue California skies, in which the wind would subtly blow and the earth would imperceptibly spin, the cloud mass above changing gradually, shifting in largely unseen ways, until suddenly the whole cloud was entirely different. Something else altogether.

The loss of his mother was, by itself, an altogether wrenching experience. But there formed added layers of pain, just as his mom had predicted: the sharp sting from the established medical community's failure, followed by the unconscionable act of a heartless con artist, both of which seemed to precipitate his mother's death and vacuum up all their money. It necessarily and unavoidably shaped him. It was the first time in his life when his sense of the inherent goodness of people was shaken, along with a budding disillusionment about the world around him, where kind, innocent people just suddenly died with no recourse, as real doctors and hospitals and specialists made huge sums of money on their treatments and tests and exams, while people's lives were being snuffed out one cough at a time. His mom had suffered needlessly, he thought, while even con artists preyed on her desperation. Again, he could hear his mom's words echo in his head, but they just couldn't stand up to the mounting weight of negative emotions.

In the months and years that followed, Marco continued to seek answers, to try to make sense of things. Early on, the results were predictable. His grades in school suffered, as he showed little interest in applying himself. He turned to new outlets to help channel his dark energies. To his aunt's chagrin, he turned to reckless behavior, including drug use.

Aunt Helena even caught him with a pack of cigarettes in his jacket pocket. She crumpled them up saying, "Are you crazy! You understand why your mom suffered as she did, right?" Of course he knew. *Aunt. Helena.* That's why he did it. Maybe he would suffer too. Maybe this, maybe that. Not much made sense. He kept looking and looking for answers, as each half or incomplete answer would just give way to several more questions. As if finally discovering the right fit for a jagged puzzle piece forced him to see that other pieces were misplaced.

Along with questions about the fairness of the universe and why a loving, caring person like his mom had to die, Marco wrestled with other new issues as well. His views and beliefs about money, for example. The prospect of going to college, pursuing some great career, so he could start making gobs of money—he just didn't get it. He had trouble picturing his days chained to some crappy job day after day like everyone else just so he just could earn some stupid salary. It was money, after all, that the hospitals chewed up while making his mom miserable with toxic drugs; money that turned her into vulnerable prey for a con artist; money that couldn't save her life or keep her alive past forty years old; money that he was pretty sure couldn't make him feel whole again. Marco vowed he would never let money or its pursuit dictate any life decisions. Right now, he needed something different. Some sort of change or escape. Something that would help him fill the void, to make him feel alive again; help distract him from the constant, swirling thought of his mom's death; help cleanse from his psyche the sense of guilt that pressed down on him, adding weight to his already heavy armor of rage, disappointment, dismay, confusion, shock, and whatever else. To a large extent, Marco felt guilty about his mom's death—he felt he could've done more; could've been more attentive and noticed earlier symptoms; could've gotten another job to help out; could've helped her find an alternative treatment; could've followed up on the sham doctor, revealed him, and uncovered his lies before it was too late.

———

The accident took place because he needed the speed somehow. And needed to be reckless. For therapy, he assumed. And escape. That he could floor the gas pedal and race away from the trauma and grief and transport himself to a different realm, a different state of consciousness. He thought driving fast in his mom's old car cleansed him somehow. Filled the void. Made him feel alive and forget about his mom's death.

When she died, the Maserati became his. Marco couldn't drive it yet, not until he was sixteen, but that didn't mean he couldn't fantasize about how he would drive it when the time eventually rolled around. He envisioned open roads unspooling before him like some creature's huge black tongue, his only objective to push the needles to the right and let the giant monster swallow him and the car whole. He imagined it would be like a giant earthquake, "the Big One," as he had read about in a used paperback book he found one day while strolling along the sidewalk with his mom. It had intrigued him to the core. That he along with all these millions of people in the Los Angeles area were carrying out their daily activities and then resting their heads at night on pillows just above one of the largest fault lines in the world. He'd experienced firsthand a few small quakes, but that book had opened his mind's eye to what a truly massive earthquake would be like. Now, in the wake of his mom's death, he found himself wishing the big one would just come already and that the earth would swallow him up with it. Maybe then he could see his mom again. See her smile and laugh without pain creasing her face, cancer ravishing her insides, and both of their lives with it.

As his sixteenth birthday and driving exam started creeping up, Marco remembered the wave of nightmares crashing in on him. Nightmares about failing, mostly. But weird ones, almost comical ones. Dreams of parallel parking and literally slicing the car behind in half. Of swerving to avoid a cat and the instructor thrown from the car. Of him sneezing and then crashing into an ice-cream shop. Needless to say, in the dreams, he failed each test and had to wait an excruciatingly long time for the next shot. He absolutely *had* to get his license so he could drive. So he could escape. That slip of paper and the keys to the Maserati represented everything he valued most in the world: his freedom and independence and ability to escape from his isolated little world in LA. Also a little piece of mom left behind.

And finally he had his day, his chance to leave all those nightmares to choke on his dust and carve out figure eights in a sort of vehicular victory dance. He tossed and turned all night, barely sleeping a wink, but knew he could will himself through it. There were no parallel parking disasters, nor any incidents involving flying instructors or sneezes and trees. He passed the driving exam, and then stared for what seemed like forever at the rectangle of plastic that was his entry pass to a new beginning. *It's time*, he thought.

One day, after staying up late the night before watching movies, his phone buzzed. It was a girl he used to know and like back in LA. And now she was texting him out of nowhere. He couldn't even remember the last time they spoke. Or if they ever really spoke. She said she had popped into town to do one thing or another, suggesting they get together. Leila was her name. Now he remembered. Yeah, Leila. She even let him kiss her once in junior high, he thought. And now she was texting him. *Weird.*

Marco wasn't exactly sure what to expect when he saw her, whether she was just filling up the rest of her day while in LA or whether she genuinely wanted to see him and catch up and, maybe, who knew what else. But at that moment, when he looked down at his buzzing cell to a sudden, and completely unexpected, text from Leila, all he could do was smile: it felt surreal somehow, like in one of those dreams before his driving exam.

<<Hey, Marco, how r u honey!? I'm in town…would love to get together for drink/bite. xoxo>>

He immediately texted back:

<<Hi! Leila! Can't wait to see u. What time? I'll pick u up>>

Seven thirty was the answer, and so at 7:27 Marco pulled up to the curb of her hotel in his mom's Maserati and whisked off his former boyhood crush to the posh elegance of Nobu, of all places, in Beverly Hills. *Nobu? Why Nobu?* He wasn't sure, but swept up in the excitement, he didn't really care. Once inside, the staff in all black brought wave upon wave of buttery sushi and vinegary sweet seaweed salads and paper-thin Kobe beef and tender baby vegetables soaked in truffle butter, and seemingly to Marco, half of the entire menu, including an icy cold and silky smooth bottle of what had to be really expensive sake to wash every scintillating bite down. The two sat next to each other at a small, intimate table, staring deeply into each other's eyes and filling in the lost years, rekindling old flames, chatting about life and hobbies and passions. He hadn't thought of his mom even once. A dish of coconut and red bean and green tea mochi suddenly appeared, along with two white cups of fragrant black coffee. Before he knew it, they were out the door, breathing in deep cool breaths of late-autumn air, along with a slow dance initiated by him on the sidewalk to the sound of his accompanying vocals: *da na na na da dee do do do dee*, until the valet pulled the Maserati up to the curb next to the restaurant, and they got in and sped off through the yellow traffic light.

Leila was raving about the car. Over and over. She couldn't believe how cool it was. And stylish. And fast. And they cruised around a bit with no particular plans, going up this street, and down that street, relishing the time already spent together and all the seconds of whatever remained of the evening. Suddenly they passed a dimly lit sign that forced Leila's head to snap back around—

"Hey, was that Mulholland Drive?" asked Leila. "I've always wanted to see what all the hype was about. Let's turn around and check it out, yeah?"

"Your wish is my—" and Marco jerked hard on the wheel with a mischievous grin and slammed on the gas pedal, leaving tread marks on the road, while the Maserati carved out a perfect half circle and then shot back in the opposite direction toward the entrance to Mulholland. Peals of delight rang out from Leila in the front seat, as she turned the radio on and pushed the volume up high.

Marco slammed the wheel again and turned onto Mulholland, Leila laughing hysterically. He looked out each window, catching blurry nighttime glimpses. To the right were flashes of the city of LA all aglow. To the left, large jagged rocks a few short feet the outside of the opposite lane. There was no doubt the few sakes or some other power had emboldened him a bit, while Leila's shrieks and howls nudged him to go faster, flouting all danger and reason. And he obliged. Speed was his new companion and ally, a bond forged early from childhood fantasy and strengthened later by his need to escape the trauma, the pain. *It was his ticket out of...what?...out of...*the car shot through the darkness and gripped the bends and turns like in some arcade video game. It was as if the thick dark night and infinite blackness of the road below formed a huge cannon out of which exploded the sleek silver sports car.

Marco was locked in, ripping through every twist and turn, like it was a video game he'd played a million times before, eager only to meet and conquer the next turn, the next bend. *But shit!* A fucking hairpin turn snuck right up on him, and Marco knew he misjudged the sharpness of it, or maybe it was a slick spot on the dark road or something, but now the car spun out and flipped and tumbled—everything was unfolding in slow motion—and Marco saw his mom and cried out to her: *I'm sorry, Mom, the world let you down, I let you down somehow...I should've done more...*his guilt-stained body tossed around the inside of the car, glass shattering around him, Leila's shrieks punctuating the sound of creaking metal, and then metal on road, and finally metal on metal...*I'm sorry, Mom. I'm sorry. I'm sorry...*as the car slammed into a squat metal rail snaked alongside the road—the only barrier between them and the steep drop below to certain death...and then the rail started to give way, and the car was tumbling down...

Marco snapped awake in the hospital, breathless, with some doctor's light being shone in his—wait, no, this was his bedroom, and his bed, and he was looking at the morning sun slant through a crease in the blinds and glint off the glass on his nightstand. He was home at his aunt and uncle's. He was safe.

He took a long deep breath, trying to recall all the details of the dream. He groped for some sort of meaning in it. Why wasn't the world fair? What was he racing from? These were the first things that popped into his head. He wanted—needed—to become unweighted with this whole *fair versus unfair* quandary, *right versus wrong, good versus evil,* as the line that used to separate these things had begun to blur. Maybe he had been speeding on an uncertain path to an unknowable future, always faster and faster, like in the dream, trying desperately to escape the dark emotions his mom had insisted he needed to come to terms with. He thought about the absurdity of racing away from your inner demons instead of facing them head-on. He was pretty sure that was a surefire way to slam into a low metal rail that overlooked a steep cliff.

Hijack:
The second seat to the right of the button; generally considered to be the easiest position from which to steal the blinds in tournaments

HIJACK

"So what kind of nickname is Trigger, anyway? You were what, a hit man before I met you?"

"Ha, not exactly."

Ivan and Trigger were seated side by side on a Jet Blue flight from Miami to Las Vegas. Trigger had asked earlier for the window seat, as he always loved the last few minutes of the trip, when the wonders of Vegas magically appeared through his window like a mirage in the desert. It amazed him every time. The two young men had another hour or so before any hint of that miraculous desert mirage, or the airport, where a taxi would whisk them over to the Palms Casino. The reservation was for one room, two double beds, five nights, and, as Trigger thought, countless plans to light up the city.

Trigger added, "My moms used to say that as a kid I would be eating an ice-cream cone or walking in the park or playing catch, and then all of a sudden I could start to cry or throw a tantrum or something. That like anything and everything could trigger a sudden mood swing."

"And so she'd just start calling you that?" asked Ivan.

"Well no—she would tell my pops when he got home from work about the day's events, and he would ask her,

'So, Margaret, what was the trigger today?' And then it was, 'Where's Trigger, in his room?' And I loved watching TV shows or movies with tons of guns and action, and so when my pops started saying to me, 'Hey, Trigger this…hey, Trigger that.' I loved it…He must've seen my face light up. Then it stuck. Better than plain old Mike."

"Anything's better than plain old Mike," said Ivan, smiling and looking out the window past his friend.

Trigger too glanced out at a rumpled sheet of cottony clouds just below them. He had long dark hair pushed back under a dark blue New York Yankees cap and a trusting face, with soft features, yet untouched by cynicism or disillusionment. Ivan suddenly unlatched and lowered the tray table folded in the chair back facing him, then pulled out a deck of cards and started to shuffle. He looked at Trigger from his eyes' corners. With Vegas looming on the horizon, he could feel excitement bubbling up inside him, and knew he shouldn't say it, but couldn't help himself. "Let's do some Pot-Limit Omaha flips. One hundred bucks per flip. Quit anytime."

"Uh, OK, just a few though," Trigger agreed reluctantly. He wasn't worried about the money, as his carry-on bag's side pocket was zippered up with about thirty thousand in cash and chips. It was the simple fact that Ivan had already run up a debt with him of about five or six thousand dollars, mostly borrowing small amounts at a time, and, up to that point, had made little attempt to cut into it. But Trigger felt it was better to appease his friend early on, their Vegas trip just barely kicking off.

Ivan dealt four cards to each of them and ran out the board, with the first few flips all going Trigger's way. He sensed Ivan shifting uneasily in his seat. Ivan finally won the next one, but then lost the next four in succession, quickly finding himself in a $600 hole. Distress was etched across his narrow face.

"Hey, bud, let's just call it a day. What do ya think?" asked Trigger. At first Trigger didn't mind it: just a little friendly time-killing, trash-talking gambling between buddies. But then he caught the look on Ivan's face. It was a look that signified either panic or desperation or both, but this was the first time Trigger saw it up close, in proper lighting, and with no attempt from Ivan to disguise it. *I've seen him lose at the tables or on his computer a million times before without flinching,* Trigger thought. *Or maybe the look was always there, but I just didn't want to see it.*

Ten minutes later, Ivan mercifully waved the white flag. "OK, dude, I've had enough. Can't beat you today." He was down only three hundred dollars and was seemingly content just to leave it at that. "Tack on $300 more to what I owe you. No biggie."

"Things will turn around for you, bud. Just be positive."

Trigger had played poker and blackjack—even sports bet— with Ivan tons of times. Sometimes they won, sometimes they lost. Like everyone else. And also like everyone else during that period, they laid out money for each other without hesitation, few questions ever asked, exceptions rare. It was just the way things were done. Trigger remembered players on occasion Frisbee-tossing thousand-dollar chips across the poker table to friends who needed it to bolster their stacks. It was so common a practice that nobody would comment or bat an eye even. Things would get dicey only if there was little attempt to repay what had been borrowed. Like their situation. Which, to Trigger, seemed lately to be rapidly going from bad to worse.

The plane touched down at Las Vegas airport, and the duo grabbed the shuttle to the baggage claim, and then walked through the terminal and out by the taxis, sliding into the backseat of the first empty one. The driver had one of those scented orange Christmas trees strung on a bouncy band from the rearview mirror. Ivan, once again, couldn't help himself. "Hey, dude, you know that thing smells like dog shit, right? Fake mango scent is not exactly what passengers are hoping for when they get in a cab." Trigger winced, as he saw the driver's shocked and offended eyes flash in the mirror's reflection.

"Dude, lighten the fuck up, all right?" said Trigger to Ivan in a forceful whisper. He then turned to the driver, compelled to smooth out his friend's ruffling disturbance. "Listen, sorry man. My friend here is a bit uptight about something. He's not really himself and doesn't mean any disrespect. I apologize." *He better chill the fuck out. Or else I can only imagine what kind of trip this will be.*

At the front desk of the Palms, there seemed to be a late-afternoon shift change, making the check-in more of a hassle than it needed to be. Especially with Ivan's strange behavior, Trigger thought.

"I'm sorry, Trig. Just a little wound up is all. A drink or two might be in order—what do you think?"

"Good idea," said Trigger. "Let's drop this shit off upstairs and come back down for a few."

They made their way to the sixteenth floor, sharing the elevator with a young couple oblivious to the presence of anyone else. Once inside their room, Ivan and Trigger tossed their bags on the floor and walked over to the large windows that looked down at the pool. "We've gotta hit that spot tomorrow, no doubt, Trig."

"You think I need convincing?" replied Trigger.

Ivan unpacked some of his shirts, tossing them in the top dresser drawer, and then aligned some toiletries along the granite bathroom counter. He turned to Trigger and suggested they put their money in the safe that was tucked away in the closet.

"This way," said Ivan, "we don't have to worry about carrying around so much, especially if we're drinking or meet up with some females."

"Good idea," agreed Trigger without hesitation. "See, every now and then you make yourself useful." He opened his eyes as wide as possible and poked his tongue out to the side, the best clown face.

He had already shared a safe with Ivan at other casinos. And though he wasn't exactly thrilled with the snowballing debt figure between them, the question of trust had never been an issue. And so giving Ivan equal access to the shared safe didn't even register as a potential concern. *The dude's got poor judgment in spades,* Trigger thought, *but I know I can trust Ivan with just about anything. That's just what homeys do.*

The safe was already hinged open and empty. Trigger dug his hand into his carry-on pocket and yanked out the mess of chips and tightly rubber-banded cash. He made a cursory confirmation about the amount—*yup all $30,450 present and accounted for*—and crammed it into the open safe, in a neat pile in the back corner. Then Ivan swung around and placed the several thousand in cash he had brought near the front. Since they knew who had brought what, and kept the amounts separate anyway, there really wasn't any concern for a mix up.

"How much you got there, high roller?" asked Ivan casually.

"Little over thirty thousand. Probably won't need it all, but I think I'm gonna take some shots at the big game at Bellagio later, maybe play some 50/100 if they have it. You're OK with money, right?" Trigger looked closely at Ivan's face, deep into his eyes, trying to see if there was any lingering hint of panic or despair from earlier. He couldn't tell for sure.

"Yeah, I'm good," replied Ivan. "Just gonna play kind of small stakes for a while and try to build it up. Then we'll see." Ivan had high hopes and expectations of running up his little roll to many multiples of what it was then. "But yeah, I'm cool. Thanks, Trig."

They decided on a combination they would both easily remember and then headed down to the lobby for a drink and a bite. Chinese sounded good. Maybe play some cards in a few hours. Who knows, they both thought. And who cares—this was Vegas. No agenda necessary.

After some beef and broccoli and Szechuan shrimp, the two were eager to toss back a few vodka tonics over at the lobby bar. Ease into the night. Some sort of throwback eighties music sifted through the bar, they noticed, grimacing at each other. Since the action at the bar was pretty thin anyway, they opted to head back to the room and grab a small portion of their safe-protected stash. They'd figure the rest out later.

"Know what, Ivan," said Trigger in the lobby," I think I'm gonna head over to the Bellagio right now for a few hours. You game?"

"Um, I think I'll just hang here for a bit," said Ivan, "Maybe mess around with a few bucks on the craps table or something.

I'll probably meet you over there later. Text me and let me know what's going on."

"You sure?" asked Trigger. "OK, cool. Yeah, stop by later. I'm sure I'll be there pretty late. Good luck, dude."

"Cool. Later, Trig."

At the Bellagio, Trigger was doing what he set out to do. Grind it out for a few hours, have a friendly chat with some fellow players, and just let the trip start to settle in on him. Like the tufts of smoke permeating the room. And now his hair, skin, and sweatshirt as well. *Fucking can't believe they can smoke in the sportsbook*, he thought. Trigger glanced at the time on his phone. Eleven thirty. *Wonder what my boy is up to.*

"Hey, dude," texted Trigger, "action's real good here...you should grab a taxi and head over. I'll put you up on the board for the 5/10 if you want. Looks juicy."

"Yeah, maybe, bud," replied Ivan. "Thing is, I'm killing it here at craps...on a roll. Up like twenty-six hundred dollars. I'll put the profit off to the side and just play with what I started with. Let you know if I'm coming."

"Damn, son...nice! I'd tell you to quit now, but you can't mess with a good roll. Chat later."

Eleven thirty quickly spun into 1:00 a.m., and then 3:30 a.m. Trigger, still at the Bellagio, was marveling to himself how time just zipped by at the poker table. He racked up his chips and walked over to the cashier window. Since his last few texts to Ivan went unanswered, he was sure Ivan wasn't coming. All the better. This being the first night of the trip and having booked a small win, Trigger, now exhausted, was definitely ready to head back to the room and just dissolve into bed.

When Trigger walked in, all the lights were off, but he could still make out Ivan fast asleep on one bed, curled up like a baby with the sheets up around his ear. A few minutes passed. Since Trigger had gotten back, he had taken off his shirt and pants, brushed and flossed his teeth, even accidentally banged into a floorboard and then the leg of the night table. But he noticed there wasn't even the slightest stir from Ivan. *Must've been some damn victory celebration*, he mused. Just then, though, Trigger felt a twinge in his gut, a premonition of sorts that maybe better explained his fetal-curled, unmoving friend who hadn't responded to his last several texts, nor had budged one inch in the last few minutes.

Trigger tiptoed over to the closet that housed the safe, slid open the door with a creak, and punched in the combination to the safe. *I hope there's a big pile of dough in the front, buddy. I pray that you didn't do something stupid and blow your entire Vegas roll in one megablitz session of craps, of all things.*

The front of the safe was empty. Trigger grimaced and looked away as if punched, a cold chill spreading through him. It was like a tiny seed of panic in his gut sprouted, with prickly shoots that reached every part of his body. There was a thin light that seeped out from the three-quarters-closed bathroom door, and it obscured just enough of the safe that he couldn't tell yet if his nascent panic was warranted or not. And then another, more vicious blow. The safe—*including the back!*—was almost entirely empty except for a few thousand dollars loosely piled in the corner.

"What the fuck!" Trigger blurted out, enraged. "What the fuck did you do, Ivan?"

But he didn't need an answer. He already had it. Trigger could see the whole scenario with brutal clarity:

Ivan, swept up in the flush of excitement, dusted off the initial profits he spoke of, a rail full of rainbow chips whittled away, little by little, dollar by one hundred dollars, until he did what he assured he wouldn't do and put at risk his beginning stake too. A bad run at craps can be devastating, Trigger knew, and he could see the clear image of a tortured Ivan losing his last few chips and storming back up to the room, ripping open the safe, and snatching out every last of his dollars. Then, stone-faced, tramping back to the craps table—probably the same table; he had a score to settle after all—and making foolish and rash bets and just being utterly careless with every dollar, until the chips and cash just vanished into dust. Then Ivan would be locked in the vise grip of a biochemical madness that he wasn't strong enough to neutralize on his own, and so would float back up, disembodied, to the room and repeat the process, only now he was opening the safe without thought or judgment—seized by this stronger power that quickly slapped away notions of consequences and remorse. At first, Ivan would dip into Trigger's stash and then, still on some zombielike autopilot, snatch almost everything that stuck to his fingers—because he would get all his money back, or at least most of his own money back, or even half or so, and things would at some point turn around, and then he could just cash out, redeposit all the cash and chips, separate both stashes, and quit this despicable game forever, just as soon as he got his money back—no— just half his money back!—then he could refill the safe and live another day and try to enjoy the rest of the trip...even grind it out until he could maybe turn a profit at some point.

Trigger tried to go to sleep, but really just lay in bed with his eyes wedged shut and heart thumping against his rib cage, counting the seconds until Ivan got up so they could hash out, in detail, how he was going to repair the situation. Several hours later, when Ivan sat up in bed, it was as if Trigger were tugged on by some invisible rope connecting them, yanking him out of bed too.

"OK. So let's have it, dude."

Ivan tearfully confirmed the movie reel of absurd events Trigger had played in his head several hours earlier.

"It just got way out of control, Trig, and I'm sorry," said Ivan. "I'll try to make it right any way I can. Not sure what else to say." Trigger noticed Ivan had started packing his bags.

"This is some incredible bullshit, man! When did I ever say you could touch my cash without asking? Are you joking? You and I are done. And you're gonna pay me every goddamn dollar back."

"I know, I know. I feel like dog shit, man."

"All right, well now it's gonna have to happen this way. What did you take, like twenty grand? Twenty fuckin grand! We're gonna have a regular schedule of payments from this day on. Every week you absolutely have to pay a certain amount."

"Trigger, I know I screwed up big-time, man, but just relax right now." Trigger watched in anger and disbelief, as Ivan went to retrieve his bathroom supplies and then came back to finish packing his bags. Ivan was a picture of agitation. "I'll, um, I'll pay you back along with the rest I owe you. As soon as I can. But there's not going to be regular schedule of payments. When I can, I will. That's it. Period."

"Wait, what? No no no. I'm dictating the rules here from now on, guy. You betrayed my trust and…"

"No what?" said Ivan. "Go fuck yourself. I tried to be nice, now you'll never see a goddamn penny. Have a nice life." He grabbed both his bags and stormed out of the room, slamming the door behind him.

Trigger's frazzled brain flipped rapidly through the options: (1) run after him and beat him to a bloody pulp before the elevator got there; (2) stick his head out of the room and shout threats and vulgarities at him; or (3) compose himself and try to conceive of a way to get restitution from this prick, his former friend, whether financial or otherwise. He took a long, deep, slow breath and thought, *OK, you little snake, I'll let you slither away now. But someday you'll feel my presence again. That's one bet you can't lose.*

Low Ball:
A form of poker in which the lowest hand wins the pot

LOW BALL

"Smooth as a two-month-old baby's butt cheeks. That's how it went. Just like you taught us." Ivan chalked up his pool cue.

"I wanna hear more," said Doug Bennett. "But g'head, I'll let you focus on the shot. You gonna need it."

"OK, eight ball, corner pocket." *Whack!* "Three games to one. Rack 'em up, Mr. Bennett."

"Nice shot, young man, but you call me Mr. one more time...see the tip of this pool cue? You feel me?"

It was Friday evening at Monty's Billiards, a joint with a bar and pool tables. Miami Beach, 2014. Ivan Parker and Doug Bennett were camped out at a corner table near the back, directly opposite the bar. Several tables were also occupied, but not any of the ones adjoining theirs. For the sake of discretion mostly.

Ivan gave a mock bow. "If you'd be kind enough to rerack, Sir Douglas, so I can run the table again. Or put in a different way, the quicker you grab that triangle and set up the balls, the quicker I can give you another damn lesson on how to play this fine game. And make your daughter and my wife proud."

"Yeah, yeah, keep runnin' that mouth…and where is my beautiful daughter right now, by the way?" Doug Bennett was Ivan's father-in-law and, for all intents and purposes, mentor.

"She's out at some lounge with Val, doing her thing," said Ivan. "You know those two on Friday nights."

"Yeah, OK. So you guys got the money stashed away somewhere safe, I'm thinkin'. Somewhere no one with any ideas could get at it, right?"

"It's safer than a prom girl's, uh…whatever…*yeah*, it's safe. It's locked away in a digital safe we got installed in the apartment. Nobody will ever find it, and they'd need the combination if they did."

"OK, OK. I trust you know what you're doing by now, Ivan. Back to the actual job. You ain't really answered my question. Hold up, I'll go grab us two more Modelos, and then you gimme the lowdown on what happened."

The lights were dim except over the tables, where track lighting gave each rectangular area a nice distinct glow. The sharp crack of weighted ball against ball rang out across the room. A sign that courteously asked that you not smoke was hazed over with tufts of cigar smoke that clung to that area of the wall. Ivan had to chuckle at the irony.

Doug smacked two cold Modelo Especials on the side wood panel. He was proud of his daughter and new—what was the word? *Protégé*. That was it. His new protégé son-in-law. The evening had a good feel to it.

"OK. So?" Doug grabbed the triangle and started racking the balls, two by two.

"OK. Well I did just as you taught me—it's a dog-eat-dog world out there, *so become the fucking wolf.* I cooked up the whole operation, and it ran to near perfection. Only at the end, after almost all the chips were cleaned already anyway, did it start getting dicey, and a manager got involved. That dude Marco I brought in from the Delano got all nervous, handling his chips all strange and whatnot. So he got nabbed. Some young kid caught him. All my people were camped out there and saw and heard it all in person." He paused to chalk up his pool cue again. "Oh well, gotta break some eggs to make an omelet, right? Best-case scenario, you ask me. One fewer person I'll have to pay out."

"Wait wait wait wait wait." Doug felt a cold chill, tuning out everything after the "he got nabbed" part. Nothing else Ivan could say would matter right now. This could be a problem. "Someone on your team got caught? And what, *arrested*?"

"Yeah, but it's all good, Doug. Marco's no dummy."

"And if they offer him a deal to talk? To give you up? Or my daughter?" Doug was still calm on the outside, but felt like breaking the damn Modelo against the table right now. *Maybe across Ivan's skull.* But that's the kind of drama he hated. The kind that made you soft. What was done was done. Gotta move on.

"Doug, think about it. What could he say? I was never even seen there. No ties to me and Mon. He can't just rattle off some tale to the cops like, 'Yeah, Officer, uh, this Ivan guy I work with told me he got some chips made in China and told me'—pure nonsense. Even if he had specifics, which of course he doesn't, and was ready to rat us out. How's that gonna sound? That his boss at the Delano cooked up this great big counterfeiting chip scheme. Who knew a guy named Zhang who helped him find a factory in China to reproduce exact copies. And then set up delivery to Pittsburg, and then got driven down to Florida by his friends Don and Carlos. I mean, come on. Crazy fucking story. Who would believe a word of it? Especially when he could present them with no evidence, no paper trail, no witnesses, no money, no nothing. Just the fake chips he was caught using. He'd sound like a raving lunatic, making that shit up. Especially with my clean record and status in the community."

"So there's no trail?" asked Doug, skeptical.

"I mean there's *a trail*, there's always *a trail*, but any damning ties are stored away and about to become fish food at the bottom of the Atlantic. Literally like by tomorrow morning. In the ocean. I'm a ghost in this scenario. Me and Monica, both.

A loud *clack!* issued from a nearby table. It was two guys who were giggling like they were as high as a couple of long-stringed kites, and who showed zero interest in the discussion of Ivan and his father-in-law.

"Wait, back up. I wanna hear about this Marco dude. Then I'll decide if he's no dummy, as you say."

Doug Bennett thought back to what had landed him in the can last time. A job gone bad. People he trusted who ratted to save their own asses. He could only fuckin' hope and pray the same wasn't about to happen to his son-in-law. Boy had some serious potential. And his daughter really loved him. That he knew. He tried to think of whether there was somethin' else he could do. He didn't really need to hear all the details of the story now. He didn't need to hear nuthin'. Not once he found out someone on the job got nabbed. But he'd let Ivan speak. Pick up a few details. But just think. Should he call his boy up in Tampa? Take care of this Marco dude? Just in case? Nah, be too easy to be tied back to him. Gotta just roll the dice on this one, he thought. Hope this mofo don't squeal. And if he does, and he's actually got somethin'—some dirt or some shit—then I guess Ivan will have himself an early taste of what it's like in the pen. Don't want that for him. Wouldn't wish it on no one. *So just think, Doug. Think.* What else could be done? *What else could be done?*

"I hired him last year at the hotel. We became friends or whatever. Hung out occasionally, even had some beers, either in my office or down by the beach somewhere. So then one day I see an opening. The dude's got—Marco, that's him—so he's got this podcast blaring from his phone so he can hear it over the massive downpour. It was a Tuesday, I think. Slow morning, overcast, and then the skies just dumped on us. I already let half the staff go home and told the other half to just chill out and relax. And I get into my usual buddy mode…"

Can't believe Ivan's actually enjoying this. Gotta just let him be for now, Doug.

"…good-guy persona with this Marco kid, and I sit there and listen to this podcast nonsense about quantum jumps and whatnot. And like pretend to get into it. And then it hit me… an opening. A way in. To like sneak right into his brain like

ERIC RABIN

some evil worm or computer virus or whatever just surfing on a wave of all this quantum leap mumbo jumbo right into his cortex. The words from the podcast were the seeds that gave him the idea to do something wild or crazy. I just watered those babies a bit and…"

"Wait wait…what do you mean, quantum jumps?" Doug asked, his attention snared by the strange term. "I look like some physics professor to you? You ever see a professor with jailhouse tats like these? Break it down for me." What he really wanted to do was get inside this Marco kid's head. Maybe this would help.

"All right, OK. Sorry. Yeah, it was some podcast thing on quantum jumping—that's what it was called. Basically the guy talked about how there are all are these parallel or alternate universes all around us—based on the laws of physics, I guess they theorize or whatever—and that there's like a different 'you' in each one, and then there's certain ways to cross over into another one and alter your life…and so on. Bunch of non-sense that made my brain hurt with outright fucking boredom. But I knew it struck a serious chord with Marco. All it took then was a little prep work on my part to craft the perfect scheme and sort of weave it into the ideas of the podcast. And presto. He was in, along with Teresa's boyfriend, and we had two chip launderers."

Ivan looked over and saw Doug distracted by something. He figured maybe he should wrap up the story. Get back home. Put the computers and papers and folders in a zippered bag. Think about what spot in the Atlantic would be the lucky recipient for all the would-be evidence. Tomorrow night he could start doling out some of the money from the safe. He'd keep his and Marco's share for the time being. No need to move it yet. No rush at all. Hey, life was good. *Now where was he again?*

"Anyway, some young poker kid apparently tipped off the manager—I don't know how the hell this kid found out or could tell the difference between the decoys and real ones— but he goes squealing to the manager that he thinks Marco is using fake chips, and they nabbed Marco in the act of swapping some good ones for funny ones during a session. Then they arrested him. So that's what went down…but bottom line is almost all the funny chips were swapped or changed and then cashed out, and now we're sitting on a pretty little bundle of cash."

Doug brought his attention back to his son-in-law. "Well, OK then…prouda you guys. You pulled a nice job." *Not too fuckin' clean*, he thought, *but milk's already spilt—so what ya gonna do? Play the hand you dealt. Move on. Come on, Doug. Be cool. He needs your support right now. Give it to him.* "You deserve yourselves a little celebration time, I guess. Well done, my boy. Well done."

RIVER

Bad Beat:
A subjective term for a hand in which a player with (what appear to be) strong cards nevertheless loses

BAD BEAT

<<Journal entry for October 6, 2014>>

In my head I make elaborate plans to start over somewhere else. Just spin a globe and play *pin the tail on the donkey* with the tip of a pen. Then simply pick up and move to whatever faraway country with its exotic culture and rich history and unfamiliar foods. I imagine living very simply, working at whatever small odd jobs come my way, perhaps teaching English. Falling in love with a woman with a different skin tone and worldviews and concepts about family and tradition. I see a very happy me, stripped of all earthly possessions and lofty career goals soldered to my mind's eye since I was a little boy. Thinking of all the things it meant to be me, Marco Sharpe.

When I was younger, and traumatized from my mom's death, my therapist at the time told me to write down my feelings. Just let them pour out on the page, she would say. A way of cleansing the psyche. There are worse ways to spend my time right now, I guess. And it did help a bit in the past. So. Let the cleansing begin, I say. Woo hoo!

Sad fact: I am a thirty-three-year-old criminal, virtually broke, and a few short days away from having to live on my prick of a dad's sofa in Hallandale Beach. That is, of course, if I'm fortunate enough to avoid any jail time. Which certainly appears doubtful at this point.

Interesting fact: the term *destitute* comes from the Latin for *destituere*...with *destitutus* the past participle meaning *forsaken*...modern-day definition of *penniless*, etc.

...while the term *impoverished* comes from the Old French *empoveriss*, which is the lengthened stem of *empoverir*...based on *povre* or poor.

Additional interesting fact: the term *incarceration* goes back to the 1530s, from the medieval Latin *incarcertionem*, a noun from the past participle stem of...

Oh, just stop being a little drama queen, Marco...Goddamn it! You're supposed to just get shit out, express feelings, etc. Not write a fucking Latin thesis on tearful emotions.

OK, time to purge. Just let it out. Well, ain't life just grand. I just can't believe this is what it's come to. Never in my wildest dreams did I think I could ever fall so low, find myself so deeply entrenched in such an abysmal situation. Sure, money comes and goes, and I can accept that. But to be a fucking criminal! How is that even possible? Because I shared a fraternal moment over beers with my former boss? Is that all it really takes, one bad decision to set flames to your entire future? One little moment of weakness on a rainy day? Poof! Just like that. What was it, greed? That's not really me. A lust for excitement? What, like how I used to drive my mom's old car? I don't know. Maybe it was that stupid podcast that got me all wound up and, apparently, vulnerable to the charms of a master schemer.

I'd have to think that in some parallel universe right now, there's a Marco Sharpe, sitting on his couch, filling out a journal entry about how fortunate he feels his life has turned out, the people surrounding him, a beautiful wife and three kids, enjoying some vacation in Hawaii—twirling their little yellow umbrellas by their toothpicky stems, while they sip up the last few drops of their third piña colada. Goddamn, that would be nice. Take some surfing or scuba lessons, splash around with the kids in the water. Order pizza for the kids. Take the wife for a romantic dinner afterward. Just the two of us. That's a life. That's what happiness looks like.

Know what, I can't even blame Ivan really. What did he do essentially? What, rope me in to a profitable, well-executed scheme? I was more than happy to go along. The prospect of such easy-type money was just too alluring. And sure, he's not the paragon of trust and virtue, but…I don't know. It was really my fault, I guess. How did I get so careless all of a sudden? Why did I get so nervous? Once that kid at the tables was locked on to me so tight, why not just get up? Rack up my chips, head to the cage, and tell Ivan that I felt bad about the vibe that night. Pick it up again the next night. Christ, there were only a few handfuls of pink and orange chips left to clean anyway. We were so fucking close. *I was so fucking close.*

With destitutus as the past participle meaning forsaken…modern-day definition of penniless…

The other day, I met some woman in my neighborhood travels. She was being nice. Small talk and whatever. She said to me, "Hey, what do you do?" as I was lumbering about, staring at the birds in the sky. She did not, in fact, mean to ask if I: drive, cook, shop for groceries, clean the bathroom, tie my shoes, pee, snowboard…she meant, for a living. She wanted to know my identity.

I thought, *Well, I've recently been divested of my identity, thanks for asking.* But I mumbled out somehow, "Uh, it's a transitional period…I'm in a transition."

What do you do? What are you? What's your profession? Devastating questions right now, like daggers tearing at your organs. At such times when you have no identity. When you can't even be sure what it means to be *you.* Almost nothing. Blankness.

My self-image and self-worth are like a painting's wooden frame ripped apart and stacked near the fireplace to burn, the wrinkled empty canvas displaying my would-be identity tossed nearby on the floor. All of it to be fed to the consuming flames, as if in abject humiliation of my thirty-three years of merely a few smudges of paint.

"What are you?" she asks.

"I am the smudgy paint drips on the crumply blank canvas of life…waiting to get engulfed by raging fire. Yourself?"

And look, I hate to whine and carry on, but maybe it's just an earnest attempt—some form of therapeutic venting, whether it works or not. What else can I do? Well I guess one other option would be to speak with a specialist, a shrink. And wouldn't you know it—I just happen to have an appointment scheduled for this very Saturday morning. So that's what I'm. About. To. Fucking. Do. Right. Now.

———

"Thanks for coming, Marco."

"Hey, thanks for seeing me, Dr. Coleman. You come highly recommended."

"Well, I appreciate that. You comfortable? Can I get you a glass of water or coffee or anything?"

"Nah, I'm OK. Thanks."

Marco sat on the soft brown couch against the wall opposite the window. He could see through the glass that it was wet out again. *Raining on my parade, huh?* Marco thought, with a chuckle.

"OK, so I understand that you also spoke with someone when you were younger, a professional? After your mother died. Is that correct?"

"Yeah. For a brief stretch, when I was about ten or eleven years old. I struggled quite a bit to keep my head on straight for a while."

"That's understandable, considering how young you were when it happened. And it was beneficial, I take it. I mean, I assume you got a good deal out of therapy?"

"Sure, it's tough to come up with answers when you're young and feel alone in the world, and wrestling with a tumble of different emotions. Yeah, it helped quite a bit back then." Marco forced himself now, sitting comfortably in this new shrink's office, not to revisit those years. This wasn't the time for that. He was glad the doctor didn't press the issue.

"And is this the first time speaking to a professional since then?"

"Yup."

"OK, well, Marco, why exactly are you here today?"

"Well, my life's a complete shit show again. That's why." *Shit show*, Marco thought with another chuckle. *Funny term.*

Dr. Coleman paused for a few seconds. "Can you break that down a bit for me?"

"Oh, let's see," said Marco. "First I was arrested and charged and probably looking at some jail time. Certainly a record either way. Whatever money I had is pretty much gone. So it's either jail or my dad's sofa. Either way, my future looks pretty damn bleak. How's that for a start? Let's see...did I leave anything out?"

Another pause. "OK, well I see it's obviously a difficult time for you." And yet another. Marco could hear the patter of raindrops filling the gaps between the doctor's pauses.

"Correct."

"Can you talk about how specific events, things that happened, made you feel?" Long pause this time. "This is privileged information—I'm only asking to help you deal with matters as they stand now. Maybe help you gain a different perspective on things."

"Hey, what can I say? I did something I shouldn't have." Marco's own pause. "Something illegal. I put my trust in the wrong people maybe." He paused again...and now a stray memory shook loose and fluttered to his attention. The jazz book. It reminded him of that used jazz book he and his mom had bought on the street in LA. The one he read through, while they listened to Coltrane and the Bird. *Syncopation*, was the word. He and Dr. Coleman were a couple of jazz musicians engaged in the fine art of syncopation. "But whatever," Marco continued. "I don't wanna sound dismissive—I take full responsibility—it was my decision ultimately to get involved, my mistake. And now I have to pay the consequences. And it fucking sucks, but what can I do? Just sit here and bitch and moan about it for an hour, here with you?"

Pause. Pause. Note. "Couldn't hurt, right?" said Dr. Coleman. Pause. Note. "I definitely think it's a great first step—having taken full responsibility, owning up to your mistake. And willing to accept whatever the consequences of your actions may be. At least now, you have an idea of what's in front of you." Pause. Pause. Note. Note.

Marco thought the raindrops could be part of their trio, the steady beat on the high hat: ba tada ba tada ba da ba. *Why am I enjoying this so much?* he asked himself.

"You'll serve your sentence," the doctor continued, "if that's what it comes to, pay a fine—or whatever it is. But you *will* get through this. There *will* be a light at the end of this dark tunnel, even if you can't see it right this moment. You made a mistake, but you didn't hurt or kill anyone. You *will* get another shot to turn your life around."

"Light at the end, huh? How can you know that for sure, Doc? Maybe the light will turn out to be the bright glow from the headlight of an oncoming train. That's what the light seems to me to be right now."

Pause. "And that's of course natural for someone in the type of pain you're in. It's going to be difficult to see it as a bright ray of hope, a new start. But that's what it really is, or will be. I see too many great qualities in you for you to just give up, not turn things around eventually. And ultimately craft the type of life you want."

Drum solo…crash! of cymbals. *Well you're right on that note, partner,* Marco thought.

"Can I tell you a story, Marco?"

"Sure thing."

"In the mid-1960s, there was a particularly precocious young man about sixteen years old. Apparently not too keen on just living out an ordinary high school student existence somewhere in New York, I think it was. Well anyway, this crafty kid decided he could successfully pull off posing as a real-life lawyer, professor, doctor, and even professional airline pilot. Oh, and I almost forgot, he wrote fraudulent checks in the neighborhood of two and a half million dollars.

"As it turned out, he got caught after about five years or so, I think it was the French police who apprehended him, and he served about five years or so in prison. He managed to get released early, under conditions that he would work for the US government.

"What's my ultimate point here? Well, just that Mr. Frank William Abagnale currently runs Abagnale and Associates, a financial fraud consulting company. He is a consultant for financial institutions, corporations, and law enforcement agencies on fraud and security. A legitimate consultant and lecturer even for the FBI academy, it's been said he has serviced over fourteen thousand companies roughly to date.

"Ever see the movie, *Catch Me If You Can*? Spielberg directed it. Tom Hanks and Leo DiCaprio starred. That's the guy. Now I'm not saying you need to become some glamorized ex-con they write books and movies about—but just that if a guy who did that level of illegal activity can turn his life around to such a great extent…

"Here—I'll give you another. At the turn of the century, there was a hugely successful business mogul and icon who was convicted of conspiracy, obstruction of justice—I think it was—and two counts of making false statements or something like that. She pretty much lied to investigators about a stock sale and was later sentenced to five months in federal prison. Was that the end of Martha Stewart? Hardly. She came back with a flourish: returned to TV with the *Martha Stewart Show*, wrote some bestselling books, and did some other things that helped her rebrand her name and reputation. I'd say she's had quite the comeback.

"I tell you all this, Marco, as inspiration, nothing more. I want you to realize that this one mistake does not have to separate you from your life passions and desires, your dreams. Just keep that in mind, whatever the future holds for you."

"Yeah, I get it. I can turn things around. OK."

Eternal silence. Except for the high hat in the background.

"What do you think makes us who we are, Marco? What makes us, us?"

"I don't know. Genetics. Experience. All mashed together somehow." He was having less fun now. This was dragging on way too long.

"It's a curious blend of those things, certainly. But so, is that it, you think? We're just this hardened clay mold formed from some blueprint? Or can people somehow break free from all that and become whoever they want to be? Remember Frank and Martha? What else was it about them that led to their resurgence?"

Deep breath, and..."I guess you want me to acknowledge that even though we're certainly predisposed to certain behaviors, we have the capacity to reprogram our brains, shift our thoughts and perspectives on things. Overcome obstacles and all that."

"Exactly. Ever hear the term *epigenetics*?"

"Sure. Yeah. Maybe."

"Each gene in our DNA structure actually has like an on/off switch influenced by thought, exercise, nutrition, even trauma. Just by thoughts alone we can even control hormones and change the expressions, or in other words, turn on and off certain genes."

"So you're saying there's hope, Doc, is that it? Kidding. I understand."

"Come on, Marco. Elaborate. What do you think I really want you to explore here?"

"OK. OK. They're just thoughts, you're saying. Negative thoughts and emotions attached to them. Let's see." He closed his eyes for a second and mashed his teeth...

...Justgetthroughthisjustgetthroughthisjustgetthroughthis...

"I had a really dark period in my youth that I could've let consume me. Instead I chose to listen to my mom's advice before she died. I was a bag of jumbled emotions, like any kid at that age would be. To sort through these emotions and look for the light or goodness. To view people and the world with compassion, strive over and over to do the right thing. Make that behavior a habit, so it becomes second nature."

"And so," said Dr. Coleman, "was it time's passage or maybe your thoughts, insights, and perspective on your experiences that helped lift the pain?"

Silence. Crickets. Raindrops. Crickets in the rain. *The end was in sight! One last push.*

"You're familiar with the saying by Lao Tzu?" asked Dr. Coleman. "'The journey of a thousand miles begins with one step.' There's your new focus."

Marco decided he should open up one last time. A last hurrah, as it were. The coup de grace. "You know, they told me—down at the police station—they told me they might cut some sort of deal if I gave everyone up. It might or might not prevent me from doing time, but then I'd have to worry about possible retaliation from the wrong kind of people. People I just wanna wash my hands of, hopefully never see again. People you can trust when things are going well, but, in situations like these"—Marco shook his head for a few seconds—"the type I'd have to fear. Retributions of some sort. I'm not making any type of deal like that. I can't just live out my days looking over my shoulder every damn where I go. I'll just do my time or whatever it is. Then, like you said, maybe get out and, who knows, start a business or something. Maybe a tour of seminars on counterfeiting. Maybe even star in my own Hollywood movie."

Marco looked over to Dr. Coleman with a half smile. The two shared a laugh. Doctor and patient. Shrink and shrinkee. Jazz duo extraordinaire.

"Well, Marco, I think you're now seeing things from a healthier perspective. One in which you realize this isn't the end for you. Just a bump in the road. And despite that, you can try to use the time as productively as possible. Read or study. Write, maybe. Whatever it is that interests you. Work on that Hollywood script you're gonna star in." Dr. Coleman thought this was clever enough to laugh on his own.

"You're OK, Doc…thanks. This helped a lot. My first step in the one thousand miles. Looking forward to just putting one foot in front of the other." *Almost there, buddy. Almost. There.*

"Well, I couldn't be happier. Stay dry, Marco. And take care of yourself. Also, feel free if you want to schedule another appointment with Nancy at the front."

"Yup, another appointment. Will do. Sounds good."

Ba tada ba tada ba ta ba. Crash!...

The. Performance. Was. Over. Standing ovation. The crowd goes wild...

Oh, I'm sorry, Ivan...I didn't ask if you even liked jazz... maybe you would've preferred something with fewer offbeat notes and pauses...something more rhythmic, less improvisational? Know what? I should've been a little more considerate with your time. Anyway, was the sound quality OK? Did I enunciate enough? I mean, they are your bugs. Just wanna make sure you got what you paid for. Overpaid for, but let's not split hairs at this point. Whoops! I just realized...maybe you weren't aware yet. You even check your safe lately? Oh, course not. It's only Saturday morning. Tuesday and Saturday evenings you do inventory checks, right? Well...ta ta...good luck in jail, pal. See ya around. Arrivederci. Au revoir. Ciao. Hasta luego, motherfucker. Don't forget to write.

Ooh! One last thing...did you like the little inside joke I tossed in my journal entry? You know, the one about painting being ripped apart...That was for you, buddy. Oh, don't be coy, I know you've probably read it by now—your goofy thugs probably turned my apartment upside down as soon as I left. But no need to thank me for everything. Really. It was my pleasure. Hey, Ivan, how's this for bad etiquette after a winning hand? Ship iiiiiiiiiiiit!

Drawing Dead:
A drawing hand that will lose even if it improves

DRAWING DEAD

There's nothing like bidding adieu to both the end of a stress-ful work shift and the last moments of a successful scam with a bunch of damn poker nerds chattering about. *Why Nate chose for us to meet here, I'll never know*, thought Teresa. Nor did she care, really. The fact was that she was much better off finan-cially at that moment than she was about a month ago. Well, in theory, at least—she still wasn't in possession of all her newfound riches. Ivan had the money still tucked away safely somewhere, a wall-mounted safe maybe, one for which only he knew the combination. Or so that was the rumor, anyway. And she was quite familiar with rumors.

Teresa was already on her third tequila when Nate said, "How sweet is it that it's all over?"

She looked up at the ceiling, eyes closed, as if in contem-plation of something deeper, something Nate could only guess at. She took a deep breath in, and then went into typical Teresa theatrical mode, speaking slowly and crisply, as if on stage be-fore an audience: "Sweet as the faint, far-off, celestial tone of angel whispers, fluttering from on high."

"OK, well I won't ask where you got that one, Teresa, my love."

"The poet, William Winter, for...those...who...care."

Nate had trouble gauging his girlfriend's mood. He hoped she was just being playful. "Why again did you never pursue a career in theater or Hollywood?"

"Oh, I don't know," she said, her head still tilted toward the ceiling. "It must be you poker geeks I can't tear myself away from."

He tried a different tack. "But can you believe, T, that Sam kid? ID'ing Marco's chips? I played with the fakes for over a month and sure as hell never noticed a difference, especially in the middle of action."

"Yup he's a sharp one, that Sam," said Teresa. Her attention was elsewhere.

"Guess I'm just glad it was *his* chips that he spotted and not mine. I'm just a lucky soul these days." He found himself thinking about the day on the water with Marco. God, was he thankful Marco told him about the bugs. Nate had their entire apartment, wardrobe, and car scoured clean a few days later. He kept a few in a closed drawer, every now and then gently placing one on the counter or kitchen table, as a nod to Marco's advice about using it to his advantage. But his new buddy Marco was gone. What could he do? "It just sucks, now that I've gotten to know him a bit. Marco getting shamed like that in front of everyone. And then taken downtown and arrested. What was it? Nerves? Just sloppy? Did you notice that while dealing?"

"Huh? Oh, uh, maybe a bit."

"Hey, is there any chance this screws us? Out of the money, I mean. That Marco gives up Ivan to make a deal somehow?"

"Nope. No shot."

"How can you be so sure? Isn't it self-preservation mode for him right now?"

"Remember, Nate? We discussed this earlier? It's not worth it for him and the charming wife to make any enemies. Marco's pretty stoic. And practical. I'm sure he'll just take what's coming to him and move on."

"Yeah, maybe. Still a shame though," said Nate.

"Yup. Shame."

They spent the next few minutes in thoughtful silence, taking in the din around them. From one side, scattered conversations mingled with the overhead music and the clank of bottles against the metal bar well. From the other, worn chair legs scraped against the wood floor, as a delivery truck's back door slid shut with a roaring clack. Nate was still absorbed by how unlucky it was that Marco got caught, right at the end of everything, and he had to remind himself how quirky life and fate could be sometimes. He also couldn't help but notice Teresa was somewhere else entirely—there but not there—like a ghost... Nate sensed he probably shouldn't probe her with any more questions, as she appeared unusually pensive at the moment. Lost in her own private thoughts. *But, my Lord, is she gorgeous. She can be my silent beauty for the rest of time, if that's what she wants.*

"All right one last shot," said Teresa, breaking the silence with a new pep. "And then we skedaddle."

"Well bottoms up, then." Nate's mood was irrepressible. Life was just too good right now to not savor every damn moment. They polished off their respective tequilas. "You send for Uber yet?"

"On their way," said Teresa, with her patented smile finally making an appearance.

Once home, back in Fort Lauderdale, they kicked off their shoes and settled in, Nate taking a detour to go pee before heading back to the living room couch. Teresa was up and about, lighting a small store's worth of scented candles—vanilla bean and cinnamon spice, was it?—and by all appearances seemed to be herself again. She was staring at Nate seductively. The she reached her long fingers down her shirt and slid a small vial from her bra, waving it playfully in front of Nate's face.

"What's that, T money?" asked Nate, surprise and concern competing for room on his face.

"Oh, just a little party stuff for the two of us on this joyous occasion," said Teresa. Nate could tell her mood had perked up several notches since they got home. She added, "Ally got some for me. For us."

"Is that *coke*?" asked Nate.

"No, baby doll—this is Special K, and we're gonna do some, and you're gonna think we were in heaven."

"I already think we're in heaven, T," said Nate, uneasy. "I'm not sure I wanna do any drugs of any sort tonight. Let's just have a few more drinks and put on some music and get in bed."

"Well, I like where your head's at, my studly man," said Teresa, now behind him, rubbing his shoulders and dappling his neck with soft kisses. "And I *am* gonna put some music on. And we *are* gonna get in bed. But…first, we're gonna have another tequila and also do some of this fun candy powder, and then we're gonna have the best sex ever known on planet earth. End of discussion."

"Um…what's Special K?"

"Ketamine, dumbo. It's a sweet little high."

"But what about the drinks we've had—"

"What about 'em?" Teresa cut in, as she formed the second neat line of powder on the tabletop, to match the one she had already cut out. "It's just gonna intensify the high; trust me." She stopped abruptly and looked dead straight into Nate's eyes. This was *her* time. *She* was in full control. "Two questions: (1) Do I or do I not know my drugs? and (2) Would I ever suggest we do anything that would hurt us? Come on, Nate, baby. I love us."

Nate shuffled over to the glass table and forced himself to switch off that nagging sense in his gut or brain—or both—that was telling him this was a bad idea. Not exactly alarm bells, though maybe something close. But he loved and worshipped Teresa way too much to get into an argument over something as small as this. Plus, they clearly deserved a celebration. Drugs or no drugs. To Nate, any threat of storm clouds was well behind them, and it looked like clear blue skies ahead.

"OK…I trust you…gimme some."

"OK. Here's a line for you and a line for me."

They sat back against the beige couch's soft, ribbed cushions and let the chemicals do their thing. *Work their magic,* he heard Teresa add. A few minutes in and he was floating, his whole body abuzz with pleasure. Another line. Some more tequila. *Wow was T fucking right about this stuff,* Nate thought, soaring.

Fifteen minutes or so passed. Each moment now was intensified—but frighteningly so, Nate thought. He sensed he was becoming detached somehow from his body, viewing the entire scene as if from high above, brushed up against the ceiling. And then the hallucinations and voices set in. This wasn't some sweet little high. This was bad. Worse than bad. Everything was wrong. *What the fuck were Ivan and Monica doing there below, staring up at him? And now, Marco...*he was blasting through the front door...*and who was that? Seth? What the...*his former students...from his poker classes...all stampeding in through the door? *What the...*

Nate Daniels, you made a big mistake, my friend. You betrayed me. And now you're gonna pay...

*Marooo? Marooo, I ddnt...*Nate, despite every effort, could only answer in an indecipherable mumble.

You let me down too, bro. You should've been there for me. My older brother...

Sethhh—youwerrr...Icanttt...I ddnt...

Peter chimed in: *Yeah, we can all definitely relate. That emptiness inside, like you got blasted by a shotgun in the gut, and it's all hollow but kinda burning around the edges. And you start getting faint like all your blood's seeping out. Like someone reaches into your chest and just rips all your internal organs out in one tug.*

Then Lewis's voice overlapped with Peter's: *And like bam! It can all be wiped away with a bad card or two and like forget about floating on clouds and shit, you're all hollowed and gutted out...have trouble speaking and even breathing.*

Buuuutttt waittt, guyyssss...I donnntt...Icannttt...

Meanwhile, Teresa had her own little buzz, in part from the tequila she threw down earlier, though mostly from the intoxicating significance of this long-awaited moment. This was her time now. Her long-awaited time. Her lines were lines of sugar, not ketamine. Her tequila was in fact tequila, like the one she prepared for Nate, only hers wasn't also spiked with the remainder of the vial's odorless, colorless, and extremely potent ketamine. Nate had downed his glass in the few moments after she had handed it to him. As she had prodded him to do.

For Nate, the earlier promise of heaven had quickly become a screaming, roiling hell, his head squeezed in an invisible vise, a grand piano crushing in his entire chest. He gasped violently for each breath. The visions and voices were still there, but those concerns were now secondary to the desperate struggle for oxygen. Suddenly, he fell off the couch and landed with a thud on the hard wood floor. First there were dry heaves, then uncontrollable vomiting. Teresa, ever vigilant, quickly ran over and spun him over on his back.

For good measure, she thought. *Good-bye, Nate.*

Nate was gone. Dead. Choking on his own stinking puke.

After a tearful 911 call, fully rehearsed beforehand, and delivered with aplomb, Teresa found herself in the back of an ambulance. She was freaking out and slobbering incoherently, focused intently on emulating her favorite actresses. She envisioned some really powerful crying scenes she could draw from: Charlize Theron in *The Devil's Advocate*, maybe? Rachel McAdams in *The Notebook*? Her face was now glossy with tears, her demeanor that of a loving hysterical girlfriend, unwilling to accept circumstances as they were, wailing to the heavens that her Nate had left her. She bellowed at the EMTs, "I told him it was strong and not to take so much...but he, he just wouldn't listen...he just kept doing more and more...we were celebrating...he just got carried away...oh I can't lose him I can't I can't...no please...Nate, you can't leave me!"

————

So here I am, alone in the hospital after some sympathetic doctor just explained to me that he was so sorry for my loss, but there was nothing more they could do, etc. All I could think of at that moment were the truly immortal words from some Charlie Sheen interview I had watched on TV years back:

"Best way to not get your heart broken is pretend you don't have one."

My sentiment exactly, Charlie.

Nate didn't have to die, of course. I just thought it best that he did.

It's not that I believed he would ever pose any kind of threat or anything like that, it's just that the clock on my cold revenge on the Daniels brothers had struck midnight, and my long-suffering psyche was about to turn into a rotten pumpkin. Oh, and I could always use Nate's share of the money too. That was the cherry on top.

Admittedly, I used him for sex and companionship, I guess. I enjoy and need those things like anyone else. They're important. But from the outset, Nate Daniels mainly served as what I had planned him to be for years, the fitting object against which I would exercise all my pent-up demons. His fucking brother ruined and corrupted and stole an important part of me, my spirit, and Nate just hummed along and didn't do a thing to help me. Not only that, I distinctly remember how he viewed me on that nightmarish day, the words he used to describe me in my pathetic state. Oh dearest Nathan, of seeming purity of heart and spirit, you even helped that douche bag cover up his crime and everything. How could I ever forgive you for that?

I actually came to like him. How can you not? That handsome face, kind eyes. But whatever affection I developed was always going to be overshadowed by my dark, unswerving designs for vengeance—a vengeance *owed* to me. One I think I fully deserved. Tossing him away like a worn sex toy was an option, just to leave him shattered and whimpering—after all, it wasn't he who had *drugged*, *kidnapped*, *sexually assaulted*, and *raped* me on that oh-so-sweet-sixteen evening. But his douchebag brother is currently serving a long prison sentence for some other felony (*surprise surprise!*), and he's unreachable. And sure, there's a sense of justice in that, but not a deeply satisfying one. I didn't get to put him there. And so I certainly wasn't going to just wait around for him, twiddling my thumbs, tickling my little panda tattoo. Drugging his brother (*oh, I'm sorry, did I give him too much?*) would have to do for now. Baby steps to my recovery.

And so, while Lady Macbeth may dwell in doubtful joy, I, Teresa Reynolds, find that getting what you want certainly does bring peace of mind.

Floor Decision:
A ruling or judgment made by a supervising employee in a card room, generally in order to adjudicate a dispute

FLOOR DECISION

Paul Townsend found himself in one of those moods. The really good kind, where you want to do your best Charlie Chapman imitation with a joyous little leap as you clap your heels together. He even woke up with a certain pep. His wife got out of bed a few minutes before he did, and she woke up peppy too, and with a measure of glee that had apparently seeped from her pores, rose off her skin, and wafted over to his side of the bed. It looked like a promising day for the Townsends.

And it was because of this chipper-type attitude that the first sounds of work danced through the air and tickled his eardrums like a fine symphony. In his poker room, at the Hard Rock Hotel in Hollywood, Florida, like at countless others across the globe, there was the sound of chips. The constant, unbroken shuffling of chips—that certain rhythmic click and rattle of plastic-clay coaxed together echoed throughout the room. It had a lovely timbre, a beautiful pitch, on this fine autumn evening. Paul thought it sounded quite like a kitten's purr. Or entire litters of kittens purring. Or maybe the soft crunch of small rocks under rubber-soled sneakers. Very soothing. Quite pleasant.

To be sure, thought Paul, even sounds universally accepted as pleasant or soothing can turn ear-grating if conditions permit: a headache, a bad mood, an argument with the missus, a traffic-plagued commute, a floor employee showing up late—or God forbid—calling in sick at the last second. Then, even Mozart's Violin Concerto no. 5 itself might sound like a maddening cacophony.

But not today. Not on this glorious evening when all the pieces would finally fit together; when fortune would smile his way. Not when, in the span of several hours or so, the following events would unfold like magical origami:

A. Paul would start his shift.

B. Activity on the poker room floor would go on as usual.

C. Marco would place on the table and into play many of the decoys he'd been using.

D. Marco would ensure that someone, another player preferably, noticed that one or more of his chips was off somehow, seemed fake.

E. Paul would make sure he was the one first to the scene to handle the situation.

F. Paul would instruct that they bag all of Marco's chips and proceed to have one of the security guards escort Marco outside to a squad car.

G. Paul would calmly explain the situation to the remaining players and place a temporary play stoppage at the three big games that featured the large denomination chips, insisting that all players remain seated where they were, in front of their chip stacks, while he and other management investigated the situation.

H. Paul would then request his staff to exchange the chips that had been in action for old chips taken from a small storage area behind the cage (kept for this very eventuality), the older chips—differently colored, though of equal denominations—to be used for the rest of the night's action, until the matter at hand was resolved.

I. Paul would have Marco escorted to the police station, "arrested," and "charged" for fraud, counterfeiting, and money laundering.

J. Paul would notify the higher-ups that Ivan Parker was then to be *actually and legitimately* arrested and charged, his laundered money to be seized as well.

K. Paul would let the clamor on the floor die down, and then would personally drive to the police station to pick up Marco and take him wherever he wanted to go.

L. Paul Townsend would be lauded for all his planning and execution in the confiscation of the chips, retrieval of the laundered money, and apprehension and arrest of one Ivan Parker for both this and other unresolved crimes, a bevy of indisputable proof for which Marco had already amply produced.

M. Paul would indulge himself once again, envisioning with great detail the promotion and hefty raise that would certainly accompany the high praise he was to receive from all his superiors.

N. Paul would go home, have a celebratory glass or two of Perrier Jouet with his wife.

O. Paul would then proceed to make sweet love to his wife.

P. Paul would wake up the next day, somewhat of a *hero and (certainly) a badass*, his future quite bright.

Q. Paul would again relish the kitten's purr of shuffled chips as he walked into work the next day, a new man.

And so what that he needed a Xanax to get through the first couple of hours, until the wheels were finally set in motion. It was a big day. There were loose ends to consider still. He was already in possession of the physical evidence, dutifully supplied by Marco a few days before. *What a mother lode*, Paul mused. And to think that someone just hacked into Ivan Parker's computer and snatched all that info. Just yanked it from the airwaves. There were order forms for chips, with what just happened to be the *exact specifications* of the chips used at the Hard Rock. Delivery forms. E-mail exchanges. People in China with weird names that made Paul laugh. And a couple of guys in Pittsburg who sent the foulest e-mails Paul had ever read, though he was forced to admit to colleagues that he couldn't resist reading some of them over and over. After all, he needed a good laugh now and then like anyone else. Oh, and of course, there was all the dirt on several *other* operations carried out by this Ivan Parker guy. Real piece of work, this one. *He was going down. Hard.*

Something made Paul think of those little green bags nurses wore over their sneakers in operating rooms. More than once, Paul had wished the casino had offered those green bags for every limb, every appendage. Or, maybe even better, an industrial-size green monster bag for his entire body—a sort of casino floor spacesuit, or protective body glove against infectious disease. He felt the gambling world was just that filthy. It made him cringe to think about the grime on everything: the bacterial/viral/parasitic/amoebic nanoparticle grime. Not to mention the thirdhand smoke particles that sat on the surface of smokers' clothes. And whatever else. You couldn't see any of this. But it was all there. Like little chemical and biological ticking time bombs. Scum like Ivan was like that too. Paul couldn't see him, but he knew he was there. Just the thought of him and his wife made Paul's skin crawl; it made him wish again for a huge, green protective spacesuit.

But anyway, so, yeah, just one Xanax. At least to start Paul off. Then, maybe another in an hour or two—he'd play it by ear. Marco's demands seemed pretty reasonable, all things considered. Marco had made it clear up front that it had to look like he was caught in the act—so he could be shamed, his counterfeit chips seized right there in the open, all some grand show of him being taken into custody, with the doubtless appearance of his arrest. That Paul, and the rest of the staff in the know, had to act as if the discovery were some big, shocking surprise. That the suddenness of it was of utmost importance to Marco's ultimate safety. Paul recalled how, several days earlier, Marco had slipped him a small envelope, inside of which was a brief note and a small, though disabled, electronic microphone—one (the note explained) that Ivan had planted in Marco's backpack. One of many, he mentioned. That Ivan had him bugged and followed everywhere. Even there on the casino floor. So it all made sense to Paul. Marco wanted to protect himself, certain that Ivan would hear clearly, and that his men would see and thereby confirm, the entire aftermath. Paul mentioned offhandedly to Marco in a quick aside that the police would help debug him down at the station whenever he was ready. Though Marco claimed he had it taken care of already. *Smart*, Paul thought. *One step ahead of us.*

Yet Marco had not only laid out on the table all the details for Paul—all that glorious proof; he even gave Paul ten thousand bucks in cash as a show of good faith, along with a few samples of the fake chips. There was dirt, too, on this beauty of a gal, Monica, the wife, with a felony rap sheet that read like a *Sports Illustrated* double edition; along with her father, an ex-con with a number of colorful descriptions attached to his name and history as well. Marco had explained to Paul in private that hundreds of thousands of dollars had already been siphoned out of the casino's coffers by the use of duplicate chips during the last month or so. Not to mention the possibility of additional money from other laundering jobs. Really the only thing he didn't give Paul was Ivan's underwear size and favorite color. OK, not technically true, as they still weren't in possession of the lion's share of the money. Marco said he could only speculate as to where the actual safe was in Ivan's apartment, the one that housed all the precious cash. Something about that information not available in Ivan's computer files or whatnot. Marco said he also didn't know exactly how much was actually laundered, because he didn't have time to really study the Excel spreadsheets that were sprinkled throughout Ivan's computer. But the stolen figure was on there, at least, and it was a whopper of a number. Along with the supposed combination to the safe, which would help save time for everyone—the police, the casino, the courts—everyone. Paul couldn't believe how successful the fraud had gone for these guys. Anyway, thought Paul, the higher-ups would've been crazy not to meet Marco's demands, as he was handing all this can't-miss evidence to them on a proverbial silver platter. From Paul's perspective, as long as he knew he was about to take down Ivan and Monica Parker *and* get all the money back, Marco could play it any way he wanted.

His attention back on the floor, Paul couldn't help watching the scene unfold from the corner of his eye. He tried to appear normal, nonchalant, engaged in all the nightly duties with which he was normally tasked. Only tonight, he'd decided to circle the floor a bit more than usual. He was all tingly with anticipation and needed to work off some of this nervous energy.

He glimpsed over at Marco. Marco had explained to Paul earlier how he would start dropping subtle hints as soon as he found the right player and situation. Again, it had to *appear* like Marco got caught red-handed. That was the deal. With Ivan's crew members circling around like hawks, plus all the hidden mikes—it made perfect sense. Paul couldn't argue with logic. *But damn paranoid, this Parker guy.* Suddenly, it seemed

Marco found his foil in seat eight, over at table seven. *Good choice, Marco.* Sammy was a rounder. Real keen eye. It wouldn't take too much to get him to notice some small detail that would take others longer.

During one of his floor rounds, Paul noticed that Marco spotted Sam staring at him. Really eyeballing Marco and the way he was handling his chips. *Ah, quite clever,* thought Paul. Marco's forehead looked sweaty, as he kept fumbling with some of the pink and orange chips. Then he went to the bathroom. Then he came back. Then he added a few chips on his stack. All of this was permitted, of course. But, then again, Paul wasn't about to say anything about anything. Not on this night. Oh, and then Marco losing that one pot to Sam. *Very nice.* Paul knew it was crucial for the first domino to fall, which would thereafter kick off a series of perfectly planned, finely scripted minireactions and events. *I gotta say,* thought Paul, *the duplicate chips did look damn good. Ivan, I'm certainly impressed with your attention to detail.*

Paul missed a bit on the next loop around the floor, but did pick up on one glaring thing. There was some guy out of place. He was leaning against a post, sipping at some pink-tinted beverage through a straw, pretending to watch TV, but really keying in on the action at table seven. And on Marco, specifically. Was this one of Ivan's goons Ivan sent to follow Marco? Seemed like it. The guy had small, well-formed features on what was an almost shockingly bright red face. Even in the dim lighting, Paul could see that. It looked to Paul as if his skin were a smooth strip of pale leather, first stretched and sunburnt, then finely creased. Grayish, brown hair, thinning and neatly swept back against a slight hairline recession. To Paul, the guy was like some movie character he knew well. Jon Voight! This was Jon Voight in a movie. In Paul's Oscar-winning movie! Though not the real Jon Voight, but one who had fallen into a long, unprotected slumber under a scorching desert sun, only to wak...

He snapped his attention back to the table. He was *certain* he'd seen Sam playing a hand blind—he didn't even look at his cards! And now...and now...in a big pot with Marco! *This could be it!* Excitement and anticipation bubbled inside him now like the effervescent ginger kombucha he loved to drink in the mornings. He knew his moment of greatness was almost here. But then...was somebody kidding him? Goddamn table two suddenly requesting a ruling on a hand—*it had to be right fucking now!*—and Paul had no choice but to go, as he turned and trudged away like some pouting child. But then...but then... yes, he was able to catch the tail end of the hand: Marco and Sam were now heads up, a sweet little pot, slowly building, like some tumbling, color-stained sand dune of chips, its sides spilling over in the wind...like some beautiful pile of rainbow confetti (this was soon to be Paul's celebration party, after all)...like some...like some...oh, and now Marco was putting on an acting show, but oh what a show it was! So subtle that Paul couldn't really even call it acting...it was more like... more like...but then...and then...*Was Sam buying this all? Did he think it was genuine?* Paul wanted to jump up and down and stamp his feet, almost apoplectic with childlike glee.

Instead, Paul decided it was altogether necessary for him to just drift off to the room's corner, slowly regain his composure, breathe a bit, and give Sam free reign to carry out his all-important role. To light the fuse on the ten thousand roman candles of Paul's future. To...to...*was Sam now weighing a chip in his hand, holding it a weird angle? Did he even just scratch the surface of it? Yes, he did! With his fingernail! Sammy, you keen eye, you!*

Before Paul even had time to completely gather himself the way he wanted, Sam was up from his seat, now walking over to him and calling his name. *Guess it's time to make that call*, thought Paul. Eyes closed. Deep breath. *We can do this, we can do this, we can do this!* Another deep breath. Eyes wide open. *Let's do this. Let's do this. Let's do this.*

Slow Roll:

To delay revealing a strong (and likely winning) hand at show-down, in an attempt to force other players to show their hands first; whether done intentionally or not, slow rolling is considered poor etiquette for giving players false hope of winning a hand.

SLOW ROLL

"Misdeal. It's a misdeal."

Ivan told me that story once over Tecates and fresh guacamole, prepared tableside. It was a damn good story. Highly entertaining, really. I must've tossed down like three beers and an avocado farm's worth of guacamole, plus God knows how many chips, as I sat back and listened, rapt with interest. Some storyteller too, that Ivan Parker.

Anyway, so *misdeal*. There's several possible reasons for one, but if the dealer calls misdeal, it means the current hand is considered dead, or over. The cards are thrown back, and a new hand is dealt. Play resumes as usual. It's a momentary blip in the action, really. Nothing else. And for me, that's all the few minutes scribbling a stupid entry into some imaginary journal amounted to. A mere blip. And another few minutes chatting it up with a friendly jazz-playing shrink. Just a blip. And now, it's a new hand:

…The cards have been dealt. Marco Sharpe, on the edge of his seat, scoots his two down-faced cards closer toward him, tucking one neatly under the other so their edges lie uniform. He then gently lifts the bottom card with his thumb and snaps the top corner back with a

sharp flick, as his head tilts down to peek underneath...an ace! The ace of clubs. Good start, ladies and gentlemen. Marco swiftly slides the top card now to the bottom. Their borders lie flush with each other once again. This time he nudges the corner up and pushes it back ever so slightly, squeezing it slowly, gently, pinching it with the tips of his first two fingers, as if about to rub off a tough smudge with the heavy friction from his thumb. Now he angles and leans his body to the side and tilts his head even lower than before, almost falling over and out of his chair, straining to get an early glimpse—not a definitive look yet, just a glimpse—at what might just be...could just be...and yes, in fact, is...another ace! The ace of hearts...

"What are you?" asks the woman on the street.

"Oh, I'm just a guy, holding two aces, looking to take down the monster pot of my life. Yourself?"

———

I'm on a plane now. I'm in first class, on an American Airlines flight from Miami to—*whoops!*—almost spoiled the fun too early. We'll get to it soon. So. I'm on a plane. I'm in first class, soaking in the cottony spread of puffy, orange-tinged clouds outside my window. I sigh a mountain-size sigh of relief. Kilimanjaro-size. The end point. I can actually see it. Touch it almost. Taste it. When I can take off this ridiculous veil, end this charade, drop the curtain on this song and dance, call it quits on the dog and pony show—and shed this pitiful character. Flip the switch to the real Marco Sharpe again. Plain old lovable me.

Surely by now, Ivan has read my journal entry (the one I left in plain sight for his flunkies to swipe from my kitchen table). And I'm absolutely *certain* he's already listened to the transmission of my session with Dr. Coleman. Why would he ever want to miss out on that hour of psyche-squeezed treasure? (Oh yeah, I couldn't just toss away all those lovely little hi-tech bugs without extracting at least a *little* benefit from them. I knew they'd be good for something.) I'm pretty sure at this moment he'll be content with the thought that it wasn't me who ratted him out. Or swiped the money. That surely Nate was somehow involved. And wasn't really dead, but just vanished. Or that maybe it was another insider in his crew. Don maybe. Don knew all the details. Ivan won't suspect me, not for a little while anyway. Maybe ever. How would he ever find out? That's what this whole final act was, by the way—insurance on my part. Keep him off my scent just long enough for the cops to pick him up at his apartment. Or wherever he's slithering around when they find him. How fantastic would it be if seconds after he opened his safe and discovered it empty, the cops came to bust his ass? It would be like watching Ali pound him with a heavy right, bloody pieces of tooth and lip shooting out from his battered face, and then steps in Mike Tyson, just laying into the bottom of his chin with a vicious uppercut, his neck snapping in two. *Pow! Pow! You're out!* Or... maybe it just buys me some time. I'm not overly concerned at the moment. Ivan's got bigger fish to fry right now. Some major legal battles to contend with. I can only assume he'll be tied up, preoccupied for a while.

Maybe at some point he'll gain some clarity. Put some of the pieces together. *Yeah, I guess it still could've maybe been Marco, but how could he have done it? What about the arrest? And the journal. And the audio from the mikes. And now he's gone.* Who else would he look at? Nate? Well, he has unfortunately passed away. Teresa? It seems she's disappeared too. Distraught maybe from her lover's overdose? Who's to say. What about Trigger? You know, the guy he screwed over, but hasn't seen or heard from for a million years. Nah. He's just some distant ghost. Right? There's this strange thing about ghosts, though. They always seem to come back to haunt you. Ivan surely has no clue about Trigger's involvement. Or his extraordinary computer-hacking abilities. Ivan doesn't know that this vengeful ghost (though I find him quite the friendly guy) from his distant past had vowed to return to get what was owed to him.

I love that line Ivan fed everybody. He even rattled it off to me behind closed doors one day. Looked me straight in the eye and said there was *absolutely no trail* that could lead back to him. Just so I was well aware of what was what. Or something to that effect. Oooooh...speaking of spooky. *So scary, Ivan. Spine-chilling.* Of course there's a trail. There's always a fucking trail. Just gotta know how to find it. And not only was there one, and one that we delightedly turned over to the Hard Rock and the authorities, but he had left for us a number of other footprints as well. The info on his computer was like the damn digital Appalachian Trail, for Christ's sake—all sorts of riveting details and exchanges from past capers and such, winding out in different directions, but ultimately leading back to him.

Oh, the things that a talented hacker can pull from a twisted, scheming criminal's computer. It would just blow your mind.

One of my favorite details yanked from Ivan's computer was the purchase order for the China chips we ended up using for the laundering operation. An order placed by one Joe Stein. Nice dummy name. Though I think you'd have to admit, Ivan, it's kind of funny: a guy donning a plumber's outfit who ended up hacking into your computer, breaking into your apartment, and swiping all your money. A plumber named Joe. Come on, bud. That's funny, no? I mean, I realize you're up shit's creek and all, but that doesn't mean you should completely lose your sense of humor, right?

But, yeah. Trigger. Poker player. Hacker. Nice guy. He got it all. The purchase order, with all the specifications. Info on the payment for shipment, and when it was sent and received. Delivery options and details. Certain specified arrangements in Pittsburg, detailed in full. E-mail exchanges with Don about setting up a wire transfer to the Bahamas. And the last e-mail that I thought particularly epic: "Don't fucking worry, Don. This computer will be resting comfortably at the bottom of the damn Atlantic Ocean in a few weeks...fish food, I'm telling you. Remember, dude—this is just some dummy e-mail address anyway." It's really too much fun right now to talk about—I feel like I could rehash it all day. Well maybe if my mind weren't so preoccupied with the life awaiting me on the other end of this plane trip across the Atlantic...

OK, here you have it. The truth is, I've schooled people in poker for years, at least a decade before I even met Ivan and his crew of misfits. I'm not broke. Quite the opposite. I'm flush with cash. You think I was about to go out of my way and clue him in to this knowledge? Right from the get-go, as soon as he hired me at the hotel in Miami, I saw him for the schemer and distrustful scumbag that he was. We'll call it a strong read. I just needed to kind of feel my way around the situation. Plus I figured I'd try to make a few bucks while I killed some time. I had some important life decisions to mull over, after all.

Oh yeah, so the job at the Delano was for show. As in, to show some income statements, so I could eventually open the spigots on all my barrels full of cash and let the house shopping begin. All the money I was making in the casinos playing poker over the years. Well, and of course, along with most of the chip-laundered stash now in my possession. *Our* possession, but I'm getting ahead of myself.

It's not that I don't believe in *quantum jumping* or any of that other theoretical stuff, or don't think that it can be a great motivator. But let's be honest—there's no substitute for well-engineered deceit. I mean, how far could I really have gotten with "a handshake with an alternate or parallel reality?" Handshakes are too nice anyway. Too civil. Too much emphasis on trust and civility. With every handshake you stand opposite someone ready to screw you over at a moment's notice if it suits their needs. It's like my theory on women. Most women on the planet are almost always willing, sometimes actively *looking*, to upgrade. At all times. One might love a Joe Stein (ha-ha) and his big heart and quirky mannerisms and earnest attempts at romance, but as soon as her version of a Chris Hemsworth–type comes along, she's gone, my friends. Closets and drawers emptied, bags packed, and out the door. Before you even realize what happened.

If you don't believe this, then once again you're allowing yourself to be deceived.

Take Teresa here. My new girlfriend. Or partner. Or life mate. Or whatever you want to call it. She's pretty damn amazing—brilliant, cunning, beautiful—the works. But just because the two of us ended up making a fantastic team (along with my new buddy Trigger) and ripped off Ivan and his crew without them having a *soupçon* of knowledge about it, that doesn't mean—excuse me, maybe I should say *una pisca*, which means hint or whiff of, in Spanish; it's Valencia, Spain, after all, where Teresa and I will be living in a few short hours from now—anyway that doesn't mean I can let my guard down entirely. And don't get me wrong, I love her down to her pretty little toenails, buuuuuuuuut, let's just say we have a certain understanding. A certain type of open relationship, buffered by just the right amount of mutual distrust. We'll doubtless enjoy a fantastic time together, having fun, learning the culture, *not* having children, *certainly*, *and not* getting married—*God forbid*. Hey, we both know our limits. And like I said, if you think for one moment I can let my guard down with Teresa, you're deadly mistaken. Pun intended. Sure, some may consider me twisted, but she's twisted squared, that one.

So here we are, each with a one way ticket to Spain—a place I've never been, but where I'm told, *the rain falls mainly on the plain*, and thankfully, not on the coastal city where Teresa and I will be blissfully passing our days.

Look—I know what she did. I'm not an idiot. I know it's not *Saint Teresa* we're talking about here. But I also know the gruesome details of her past. About Nate's sorry excuse for a brother. And that Nate, not completely blameless for the aftermath of the incident, really just served as some sort of proxy target for this scumbag brother. The way she describes it, Nate could have made more of an effort to help her and her situation, but opted instead to play dumb—to turn a blind eye so he could protect himself. Not to mention the degrading terms used to describe her during the nightmarish episode. And when Teresa finally put all the pieces together, she felt Nate was complicit enough. That it would've been a whole different story if his brother weren't locked away. But she was desperate to feel whole again, as she explained it. Do I agree with her decision, her subsequent actions? Uh, not exactly. But who am I to judge anyone? I don't think I'm a bad person *per se*, certainly would never kill anybody, but I was also fortunate enough to have come out of my dark past relatively intact, to retain part of my angelic light, if you will. Teresa was a tortured soul. I could see that the first day I met her. I didn't know—couldn't know yet, really—that she was mad with revenge for the brothers who crippled her innocence and youth. Again, don't mistake this for my absolving what she did. But sometimes, I guess, good people do bad things. Way life goes. I'm sure she could quote me a line of Shakespeare or two on that note.

Can I trust her completely? I don't know. How can I for sure? I'll be vigilant, no doubt. Keep my eyes peeled for signs. But for now, she's here with me, making me happy, and I her, and we're about to embark on a beautiful new adventure in a foreign land. Learn a new culture, a new language, a new lifestyle. And who knows what else.

Don't judge Teresa Reynolds. We're all flawed in our own lovely ways.

She told me recently the story of Apate and Dolos. In Greek mythology. Apate was the goddess and personification of fraud, deceit, deception, and guile. Dolos, her counterpart, the spirit of trickery and guile, and a master at cunning deception, craftiness, and treachery. I told her she might be overstating the comparison a bit, but I nonetheless appreciated the colorful reference. Hey, it's always nice to learn new things.

But listen, about this whole deception thing. I'm still that same angel deep down inside—the one my mother always spoke about. Well...almost. There's just a different version of him now. An altered version. One who's forced to still peek through the veil of cynicism, doubt, and regret. Let's remember, too, that I'm also a poker player who's trying to carve out a happy living the best way he knows how. At the tables, just like for many others in the game of life, we're given license to deceive, even get well compensated for it, generally. But, hey, if it still bothers some folks out there that someone might decide to use this skill in the real world, let's take a brief moment, shall we, to shine a cozy little spotlight on the countless millions of others who use deception as a means toward their financial (I won't even touch *political*) goals. How about the so-called professionals given a license to lie and deceive right to your face and actually get paid handily to do so? How deep does your trust lie in with these individuals?

- Public relations professionals—devoted to the professional maintenance of a favorable public image...*Image* being the operative word, not reality; not what their client is *actually* doing or has done. The job here is to manage the message, withhold information.
- Modern-day marketers—whom someone pays to create a campaign, usually about creating value...Hmm. Some clever wording here, some clever phrasing there, so that nobody really recognizes its actual value. People paid to create rewarding experiences that encourage people to pay more for a product. Period. Or enhance perceptions of the value of what's there—brand value—adding to people's conscious appreciation of a brand; they create subconscious "emotional halos" that predispose people to think positively about the brand. Seems like clever maneuvering to create a false value to me. Deception, in other words. Plain and simple.
- Advertisers—experts in deceptive practices: manipulating pictures and images to make their clients' products seem more appealing. How lovely.
- Salespersons of every stripe—these people live in a world of denial and conjuring; they're experts at

        withholding information about their own or compet-
        ing products—persuasive and deceptive and manipu-
        lative…just the art and skill of bullshitting, really.

- Wall Street—professionals in financial fraud, are they not? What with their excessive commissions, hidden fees, legal loopholes, subtle manipulations. Thanks for looking out, guys.
- Financial service professionals—where deceptive sales practices are the norm, along with bogus credentials, misinformation, and the like.
- Brokers—with their "churn and burn" mentality: commission-driven decision making.
- Sports/Athletes—even in our beloved sports arena, we see deception practiced at every turn: football offenses and defenses with shifting, dissembling schemes intended as tactical ploys; pitchers in baseball throw changeups and sliders to keep hitters off balance; crossovers and pump fakes and no-look passes in basketball.
- Gaming/Casinos—with all the pretty bells and whistles, promises of hopes and dreams and big payouts… built on the strength of all your lost dollars, people!

And obviously this list isn't comprehensive. So I don't know, maybe we, as humans, are born with this trait. That it's tightly coiled into our DNA, and just needs a little prodding by the right opportunity. Maybe Dr. Coleman could tell me whether epigenetics or something else applies here. I don't know. Maybe I'm deceiving myself. Nate got me all hopped up on a psychology jag, so I did some reading on my own. Maybe I'm just a victim of pareidolia or apophenia: psychological phenomena involving a stimulus, like an image or sound, in which the mind perceives some familiar pattern where none actually exists. I see monsters and ghosts and deceivers everywhere, though maybe, like the common mistake prevalent in the world of gambling, there is no meaningful pattern. That it's much rarer than I think it actually is. Though maybe not. Again, who's to say.

Know what? Even I, Marco Sharpe, can offer a well-timed quote now and then. Sure, Teresa's an outright compendium, and they just seem to spin off her lips like darts, while I typically need to cry out to Google for a helping hand. And, wouldn't you know it, I just stumbled upon this one, which seemed altogether appropriate for the occasion:

"One who deceives will always find those who allow themselves to be deceived."

Well, I couldn't agree more, Mr. Niccolo Machiavelli. What am I suggesting with this? Nothing. You weren't the first; you won't be the last. Don't lose any sleep over it.

———

Marco Sharpe and Teresa Reynolds—Apate and Dolos—stood shoulder to shoulder, wineglass to wineglass (they had opted for the Rueda), on their rooftop terrace in Valencia, overlooking from a distance the northern part of the Mediterranean Sea. The pleasant brine of the air mingled with the pungent scent of paella wafting on the gentle breeze from the stove inside. Teresa peered in, considering whether it might be ready or for another stir. She turned back, deciding it could wait. It was just too beautiful out there on the balcony. Too perfect. And she was really enjoying this white wine and Marco's presence and warmth by her side. She couldn't help but smile. A big, fat American expat smile, delightfully soaking in the dazzling beauty and tranquility of the panorama spread out before her.

They had decided on Valencia for a million reasons. Because it sat on the Mediterranean coast just three hours east of Madrid and three hours south of Barcelona. Because of its mild climate, with locals boasting it had more sunny days than any other city in Spain. Because of its long urban beaches lined with busy restaurants and cafes; its narrow cobblestoned or tiled walkways, with the typical laid-back European feel; diners seated outside, enjoying coffee and pastries. There was also its charm, the fine sand and clean water, the vastness of the sea it bordered, and even the beauty of the mountains nearby. How it was said to blend cosmopolitan Mediterranean flavor with a distinctly modern Spanish spirit. This was the potpourri of selling points whose beckoning scent had seeped into their consciousness from as far back as they could each remember.

They were also both moved by the city's history, how it transformed its appearance over the years while rescuing monuments that stood as witness to past eras. It was claimed that visitors could feel the pulse of many centuries in its walls and under the ground, a fact that had certainly not escaped their attention. After all, Valencia was a trading city originally founded by the Greeks. Teresa and Marco couldn't help but accept that maybe it was some sort of twisted fate that the re-incarnations of Apate and Dolos were now drawn by a kind of ancestral pull. It certainly seemed to them like fate, anyway.

For the interior of the villa, they had decided to keep the stylish, modern decor of the previous owners. This included the plush, low-slung gray couches and large, wall-mounted plasma TV in the living room, the sleek kitchen table made of some indescribably beautiful mass of lacquered driftwood, even the Spanish and Italian art sculptures that accented the living room. Out there on the balcony too there were treasures they had inherited. The long, low white lounge chairs that stretched out sleek and streamlined like perfect ice sculptures, only—as Teresa so cleverly pointed out to Marco—that *you melted into them* and not the other way around. Even the fire pit in the center was perfect. The gas spout poking up from beneath a pool of volcanic black rocks, rimmed by green-tint-ed, crushed glass sheets, the dancing blue flame caught in the crystalline layers, a visual splendor to enjoy while it warmed your bones. She had been the balcony botanist/architect, lin-ing the terrace with numerous flowers and plants—lilacs, peo-nies, gardenias, carnations, and Spanish bluebells (and many others Marco didn't know by name)—a welcome pop of color to accent the pristine marble tile and white walls and chairs. This was their home now. The result of meticulous planning and perfect execution. So now, if Teresa wanted to overindulge in colorful flora to line her stunning balcony, she would do just that.

Several months back, neither could have envisioned their lives to this point. Teresa really hadn't looked far beyond her quest for revenge to feel whole again, and now that she had attained that goal, could only reflect on what a gigantic relief it was to put that part of her life behind her. She always viewed Marco as some sort of star lead in a big production she was watching play out from the audience. She would study him, his movements and mannerisms, and of course she would at times project herself into the female lead opposite him. But she didn't think it would ever really materialize that way. She too had her concerns about trust and deceit, but, as Marco so eloquently put it: they couldn't just spend their entire lives just holed up in a cave, abandoning the concept of trust forever. And of course when they finally hooked up, and Marco painted for her the indescribably pretty picture of a life together in Europe, she struggled to come up with any compelling reason against it. Marco knew he'd end up overseas if it all worked out, Europe certainly, but not necessarily here, yet he could only hope Teresa would be on board with it. Once he'd discovered that first mini mic in the fabric of his backpack—skillfully slipped in, and virtually undetectable—he knew what the endgame should be. If Ivan wanted to get cute with him, well then Marco would show him cute. He would hear about Marco's undying trust and loyalty to both Ivan and the job's successful conclusion. He would hear how Marco planned that he alone would go down with the sinking ship, should it come to that. That he was fearful of any reprisals should anyone discover he had informed on them.

Ivan would essentially hear what Marco needed him to hear, nothing more, nothing less.

To Marco and Teresa both, the trip overseas and acclimation to a new country and culture had gone even more smoothly than they could have ever imagined. Forget about the typical easing in, they thought. You don't just inch down the crags in the side of the cliff and then wade into the water toe by toe—you dive *exuberantly* off the cliff and plunge deep into the water below. *That's* where the real fun and excitement could be found. There, on the balcony, Marco and Teresa were enjoying a welcome respite after a week of cultural indulgence. They had walked and biked and hopped on buses, forging new paths through their new city, drinking in the beauty of art and architectural history, savoring local delicacies. *A truly surreal experience*, they both agreed. Though maybe a bit more than they had anticipated it would be...

They recalled the morning of that first day. To her, it was *act 1, scene 1* of some acclaimed five-act production, Broadway maybe, or ancient Greek theater, or wherever, playing out just for them. The curtains opened, the characters and backdrop slowly revealed. Scents and sounds were pumped in on cue. Bit players made their occasional well-timed appearances. Teresa's performance felt effortless, routine. She imagined having rehearsed her lines so many times in her head that it just flowed, as if perfectly natural, almost improvised. Gestures of wonder and awe and surprise, all acted out as the normal responses of an actual person—*though it seemed so unscripted for a play...*

For him, it was a like some *feverish dream* where everything rolled out in a blur. But this time, unlike in his childhood nightmares, it was a blur of sheer contentment. Images came and went, flashing before him, sometimes getting snagged in the periphery. But there was another difference: it was a sort of *lucid dream*. He was aware of his place in this dream—aware of the countless shapes and shifting forms, the play of shadow and light, the new faces and objects. He could only ask himself at various intervals—*Am I really here?* And yet, he still couldn't be sure. He almost couldn't remember the events leading up to it, or even why he was there, as if he were just watching himself and Teresa from a distance...

Act 1, scene 1. And the opening of the dream sequence. It started slowly, calmly, unfolding gradually. They had stopped by a small local cafe, fueling their makeshift itinerary with coffee, alongside ice-cold, milky horchata de chufas and fartons. Teresa got a good belly laugh at the name of the pastries, those used to soak up the horchata. She wasn't thinking in Spanish yet—and wouldn't for some time—so the first thing she saw on the menu was *fart ons*...but they were delicious, they both agreed, somewhat less sweet than a doughnut, though not quite as bready as a roll. But sugar dusted, they turned out to be the perfect accompaniment to the horchata. Sort of like Teresa, Marco (a sprinkle of sugar on his lip) had opined, much to her delight and amusement: *less delicate than an orchid, not quite as thorny as a rose.* It earned him an horchata-stained kiss anyway...

And cut to scene 2, as the stage setting turned over, and new characters were introduced (for her), along with next dream sequence (for him), as time seemed to compress, and images and bit players started to meld together...

...first in Old Town, where they got lost within the old city walls, wandering along narrow cobblestone streets and crooked paths...as fig trees and spreading palms pocked the courtyard. There were massive fifteen-foot-high wooden doors with elegant knockers and hinges, and wrought-iron balconies from which geraniums spilled...the whole layout seemed to them haphazard, unplanned—but breathtaking...churches and Old World palaces that sprung up out of nowhere or were hidden behind plain white walls...an intricate network of streets and alleys left over from the past...pedestrian zones where restaurants spread their tables outside their doors, and accordion music filled the air...boulevards of flower-filled tables, colorful umbrellas, and animated crowds of locals enjoying drinks and tapas...soaring church towers, ornate museums, bustling markets, and vestiges of the city's grand gateways...

...and then over to the Gothic thirteenth-century Valencia Cathedral, built on the site of an old mosque, as they were told—Teresa was struck by its concave shape and its disorienting effect—she even felt compelled to mention that *maybe they were actually dreaming*...the structure bursting with fifteenth-century paintings. She and Marco shot up the stairs to the top of the cathedral's octagonal bell tower and marveled at the bird's-eye view over the red-tile roofs of the city...as Marco nudged her to look toward the sea, the modern museum district in between.

Another backdrop change—was this act 2 already?—the scenes rushing by more quickly now...they found themselves in the National Ceramics Museum, having climbed down from the bell tower and shuffled over the twisting cobblestone paths, where there shone a splendid collection of ceramics and other artwork, with several Picasso ceramics on display...then to a room recreated as a Valencian kitchen, covered in the region's famous tiles...as they ambled down an alabaster doorway, past frescoes, painted ceilings, crystal chandeliers, marble staircases—*Marco musing how there was just way too much beautiful detail and texture and light and color for it to be a dream*...

...now at the Old Market, center of commerce for centuries, as the locals explained...they saw the wealthy and poor, fashionable and frumpy, all shopping side by side...inside a huge building that looked like a railway station decked out with ceramics...the air fragrant with smells of pungent olives, sweet fruit, fish, and dried sausages...a constant clamor filling the air as children squealed, vendors shouted prices, cell phones chimed, and fishmongers slammed their rectangular knives against cutting boards to kill their squiggling eels... Marco and Teresa looking down suddenly and finding themselves dining on grilled squid and roasted pumpkin, washing it all down with several "Water of Valencias"...like mimosas with a real kick, they both agreed...

...then flashed across the street to another market...a hall of slender columns that rose majestically to an arched ceiling above the Lonja de la Seda or Silk Exchange—a friendly local explaining how it was once the center of the Mediterranean silk trade, back in the fifteenth century...its elegant calm contrasting with the cacophony from the other market...gorgeous churches...majestic doorways surrounded by intricate Gothic carvings of bawdy scenes. Teresa pointed out a gargoyle on the corner of the building above the patio filled with orange trees—a buxom woman—while all the other gargoyles were monsters. She and Marco cackled in delight at the imagery...

...suddenly transported somehow to Museu de Belles Arts de Valencia, or the Museum of Fine Arts, with its large collection of paintings from the fourteenth through the eighteenth centuries. There was Velazquez, el Greco, Goya...then the couple swooped over to the Valencia Institute of Modern Art, with its abstract art of the twentieth century...then outside the medieval center...to the ultramodern City of Arts and Sciences, designed by Santiago Calatrava—they were told—with its huge and beautiful cultural and architectural complex...an amazing display of Mediterranean art...an aquarium where they walked through underwater passages...a futuristic science museum, housed in an eye-sloped auditorium with an omni theater...

...finally, a short saunter to the beach and harbor...wide, sandy beach filled with locals and packed with restaurants... crowds spilling out into the streets. They went in and ducked under the bar and sat in a small room at one of the handful of raised tables, surrounded by massive wine barrels...large pans floating by of traditional Valencia paella with chicken, sausage, and rabbit...others with clams, mussels, shrimp, and fish...Rioja Crianza vino tinto to wash down their own plates tumbling with succulent paella...

...*surely this had to be act 3—the climax—right?*...when they noticed it was several days later, a sunny afternoon and their first exposure to La Tomatina—the long-revered, annual tomato fight—how amazing that they happened to be there just in time for that last Wednesday in August...they couldn't believe that so many people and so many bright-red tomatoes could be packed into one small area...zipping softened tomatoes at thousands of people and getting gleefully pummeled in return...easily the most fun they had ever had in their entire lives, they agreed...this event would be forever burned into memory—now they were really Spaniards!—and they would always remember their first time...

...*and act 4, the reversal; while, the dreamlike haze also began to lift and resolve...time slowing down now.* They were back home. At the two-story villa they had purchased in cash. Their new, glittering home. They didn't own the villa outright and still owed quite a bit on it. And sure, they agreed they shouldn't be profligate with money. But, ahhh, owning a villa on the Mediterranean. This was a prospect most people could only fantasize about. And here they had it. So what was a little debt and belt-tightening, in exchange for all this splendor...

...*finally, act 5! The resolution—when, as Teresa knew, the audience holding its breath would then release it in a kind of catharsis—with Marco now snapped fully awake from his lucid dream state...*

"Teresa, my dear, looking relaxed as ever. No longer waiting impatiently to get to the good times."

"No longer need to," she responded, wiping a few stray drops of wine from her chin. "Now that I have what I want. The good times—they're here, right in front of me."

Right here, she thought. *Right now*. Right in front of her. Staring at the sea, thinking of her life and the future's infinite possibilities, no pesky obstacles standing in her way. She caught a heady whiff of paella beckoning from the pot on the stove. It sat in a huge pot. On their adorable stove. In their fantastic villa. Within this unbelievable city.

"You should get a tattoo," said Teresa suddenly, overcome with emotion. "We both should…something to commemorate our lives here. Maybe a Spanish flag or something. For you, maybe right there, high on your shoulder so it sticks out a bit from a T-shirt. It'll look like some cool red-and-yellow triangle. Prideful Spanish colors for my hot Spanish man."

"Yeah, maybe. That could work. I'll look into it."

She turned toward the kitchen. "Smell that?" she asked.

"Do I *smell* it? It's like some fragrant, deep-tissue massage for my lungs. Can I have an early sample?"

"Maybe. If you refill our glasses first."

Marco padded over to the wine bucket by the fire pit and refilled the two nearly empty wineglasses, as he shook out the last drops from the bottle. With a smile stretched across his face, he shouted into the kitchen, "Oye, amor, quieres comer ahora?" *Does she want to eat now?*

"Um, uh, pienso que sí..." she managed to finally get out, smiling one of her big Teresa-patented smiles. *She thinks so...*

"Nice!" said Marco. "Y qué te parece empezar con..."

"Hey, prick...don't push your luck. I'm learning. Now come here and kiss me and tell me if the paella tastes right."

"How about you take a bite, and I taste it on your lips? Then I get the best of both worlds."

The best of both worlds, Marco thought. *Outscheme the schemer and somehow end up with all the money and the beautiful girl. Not fair somehow? Maybe. But life's often unfair. Ask Nate Daniels. Or my beloved mom. I learned that very young. You know what? Life can be really good sometimes too. Like now—Apate and Dolos, reclaiming contact with their ancestral Greek roots, running wild in Valencia, Spain. Just remember, Marco, don't deceive yourself into believing it'll always be this way...*

AUTHOR BIOGRAPHY

 Eric Rabin spent ten years as a profession-
al poker player, including one year living
in a casino hotel. His experiences in the
gambling and poker world gave him the
inspiration for *And Sometimes They Win*,
his new psychological thriller, but Rabin
has also brought his educational experience to the table.

Rabin received his bachelor's degree in psychology from
the University of North Carolina at Chapel Hill. He is fasci-
nated by the secret motivations that drive people. Rabin has
also worked on Wall Street, studied at law school, and has
been a licensed commodities broker and nightclub bartender.

Now, Rabin is enjoying the single life near the beach in
Southern California. He loves writing, fitness, foreign lan-
guages and studying people's unique personalities and quirks.